St. Elizabeth's Children's Hospital, London

Dealing with sick kids can be heartbreaking,
funny and uplifting, often all at once!

This series takes a look at a hospital set up
especially to deal with such children,
peeping behind the scenes into almost all the
departments and clinics, exploring the problems,
treatments and cures of various diseases,
while watching the staff fall helplessly in love—
with the kids and with each other.

Enjoy!

Gill Sanderson is a psychologist who finds time to write only late at night. Weekends are filled by her hobbies: gardening, running and mountain walking. Her ideas come from work, a son who is an oncologist, another son who is a nurse and a daughter who is training to be a midwife. Gill first wrote articles for learned journals, and chapters for a textbook. It was her husband, an established writer of war stories, who encouraged her to try fiction.

A DEDICATED LADY
Gill Sanderson

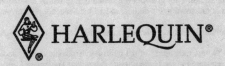

HARLEQUIN®

TORONTO • NEW YORK • LONDON
AMSTERDAM • PARIS • SYDNEY • HAMBURG
STOCKHOLM • ATHENS • TOKYO • MILAN • MADRID
PRAGUE • WARSAW • BUDAPEST • AUCKLAND

HARLEQUIN BOOKS
225 Duncan Mill Road, Don Mills,
Ontario, Canada M3B 3K9

ISBN 0-373-63173-1

A DEDICATED LADY

First North American Publication 2001

Copyright © 2000 by Gill Sanderson

This edition published by arrangement with Harlequin Books S.A.

® and TM are trademarks of the publisher. Trademarks indicated with
® are registered in the United States Patent and Trademark Office, the
Canadian Trade Marks Office and in other countries.

Visit us at www.eHarlequin.com

Printed in U.S.A.

PROLOGUE

Lucy still couldn't get over American breakfasts.

She served the usual fruit juices and cereals. The men liked the porridge she made with cream, but they called it simply oatmeal. Some preferred a maize version, called hominy grits. She cooked a vast fry-up, and made lots of pancakes—every man needed a five stack on his plate. Who but a barbarian would pour maple syrup over his fried eggs? And the amount they ate!

There were twelve men in the little hut, and she was kept busy pouring coffee and making fresh toast. But not for long. The men ate quickly and filed out, their cleated boots rattling on the ply floor, picking up their hard hats from the pile by the door.

'Bye, Luce.'

'See you later, sweetheart.'

'That was real good.'

An amiable chorus of goodbyes. She knew them all now; name, family history, character and what each liked to eat. As the only woman in camp and a sympathetic listener as well, she heard a lot of stories. Now she stood in the hut doorway and waved to them as they trekked over the rough ground to where the two four-wheel-drive trucks were waiting. A roar of powerful engines and they were gone.

Washing up wouldn't take long so it could wait— she was entitled to a ten-minute rest. She made herself some fresh toast, and a small pot of Earl Gray tea.

Then she went to sit on the steps outside, to smell the glorious air and gaze at the tree-covered mountain slopes.

She had been in the north-west of America for nine months now, and she loved it. It was so different from England. There were the distances, the solitude, the sheer beauty of the country. A chillier breeze swept her, and she shivered. There were the dangers too. She looked appraisingly at the sky as she had been taught, and there was the dark line that said a rainstorm was coming their way. The men wouldn't like that. Logging was a dangerous trade at the best of times; bad weather made it ten times worse.

The first few drops of rain banged on the tin roof as she walked back inside, and within minutes the rattle had turned to a deafening drum beat. Through the window all she could see was the greyness sheeting down.

There was a dishwasher, of course—this camp had every possible aid, power supplied by a diesel generator. Efficiently she stacked the dishes, then brushed down the dining room. The team would be back for lunch: soup, hamburgers, salad. Logging was tiring work; they all needed the energy.

'We could do without this weather, we're behind schedule. Any chance of a coffee, Lucy?' It was Jerry Zane, the camp foreman. He stood just inside the door, shaking the rain off his long stockman's coat.

'You know me, there's always coffee, Jerry. Shall I dig you out a doughnut?'

'Sounds good. With cinnamon?'

'Coming your way.'

Jerry sat at a table, produced a set of sheets of paper from under his jacket and set them down. He reached for the coffee and doughnuts she placed in front of him, and pushed the sheets towards her. 'Order forms for next month,' he said briefly. 'You're doing all right, so fill in what you want on the food section and I'll see to the rest of the order.'

This was what she liked about America. If you could do the job you were invited to get on with it. She had worked as an assistant cook at a larger camp for three months. The boss had liked her work, recommended her, and she had got this, her own cookhouse, on a month's trial. She was now in her fourth month and she thought she was doing a reasonable job. Not bad for a twenty-one-year-old girl.

'Didn't see Pete Lynch at breakfast,' she said casually as she ticked off an order for an astronomic number of steaks. 'Problems anywhere?' Pete Lynch was the paramedic. Royston Rogan, the owner of the logging operation, insisted that each of his camps had a trained medical man within at least a couple of hours' drive. It wasn't a legal requirement, but Rogan was seen as being a good, if a tough, boss.

'He took the jeep early this morning and drove down to Blue River camp. Got a call last night—someone thinks they've got an infected hand.'

Lucy nodded. Blue River camp was close—about forty miles away.

A bell rang loudly, and Jerry looked up, irritated. 'I'm not expecting a call,' he said, 'so that's got to be trouble. Be right back, Lucy.' He grabbed his coat and headed into the rain.

The radio telephone was in the foreman's cabin, and if he didn't answer an incoming call the bell outside would ring for him.

He was back in five minutes, looking more gloomy

than ever. 'It was trouble. They've had rain all night at Blue River,' he said. 'That was Pete, he can't get back direct. The road's all washed away. He'll have to drive into the next valley and come at us that way. He'll not get here till evening.'

'Not good weather for driving,' Lucy said. A road washing away was not an unusual occurrence. In fact the roads were merely tracks cut through the forest.

The two carried on working in unhurried calm. She refilled Jerry's mug, fetched him another doughnut. And the bell rang again.

'I'll get it this time,' Lucy said. 'You carry on, I've finished.'

'Thanks, Lucy. I appreciate it.' Like a lot of out-doors men, Jerry found the bookwork the most irksome task of all. Lucy knew she'd be giving him a hand later.

She fetched her own stockman's coat, pulled on her Stetson and ran over to Jerry's cabin. She knew how to work the radio—everyone on the camp had been taught to operate it.

'Big Blue Mountain camp,' she said, 'is—'

'Lucy! It's Tom,' a voice interrupted. 'We need Pete Lynch. We need him now!' Reception on the radio wasn't too good, but she could hear something in the voice that shook her. Tom—one of the men she'd shouted good morning to, not a couple of hours before—was terrified.

It was another of Royston Rogan's rules. No man—or group of men—ever left one of his camps without a radio and a direction finder.

'What's the problem, Tom?' Lucy asked, forcing herself to be calm. Getting into a panic would help no one.

'We've had an accident! It's Harry Rogan. This tree rolled and he was holding a chain-saw and he got... There's blood everywhere and we don't know what to do.'

Lucy felt sick. She had seen a chain-saw cut through a nine-inch log in a matter of seconds; what it could do to flesh didn't bear thinking about. Keep calm! 'Pete Lynch isn't here. Can you stop the bleeding and get Harry back here?'

'We'll do what we can. Will you get someone? Lucy, this is bad!'

'Just get him here. And don't hurry! We'll get things sorted.' She signed off, then ran to fetch Jerry.

So far she had found Jerry to be an excellent camp foreman. The men liked him, he knew the job and he'd work for them if they worked for him. She hadn't asked him to, but Jerry had gently told the men that she was to be respected. And he rigidly enforced one of Rogan's rules. No alcohol in camp. But as they ran back to his office she realised she'd found his weakness.

'There's been an accident with a chain-saw. Harry Rogan is cut up pretty badly, they're bringing him in.'

'Oh, God, a chain-saw! And Pete Lynch's away, we'll have to deal... Harry Rogan is the boss's brother, too. What'll he think when...?'

'That doesn't matter,' Lucy said brutally. 'A man's injured and we have to cope. Does anyone else on the team have any medical knowledge?'

'No. We've all done the one-day course but... Lucy, I'm foreman and it's up to me. And I don't think I can cope.'

Lucy had done the one-day first aid course, too. It

was good—for one day. But it was aimed simply at ensuring that an injured man stayed alive for an hour or so until a trained paramedic could get at him.

'Radio head office,' she told Jerry. 'See if they can get a helicopter out here with a doctor aboard. And you'd better give me the key to Pete's cabinet.'

All the buildings on the camp were prefabricated, brought in by the great lorries that afterwards hauled away the logs. The foreman's cabin held the radio set as well as the cabinet that contained the paramedic's equipment. There was even a doctor's examination couch. Lucy knew that the cabinet would be well supplied. But the man with the skill and knowledge was missing. She opened the cabinet and looked inside in bewilderment.

Behind her she heard Jerry talking to the radio operator at head office. 'Yes, I'll hold,' she heard him say, 'but we need action quick here.' Then, over the rattle of the rain on the roof, she heard the sound of a truck arriving outside.

She dashed out, peered under the tarpaulin covering the back of the truck. Six anxious-looking men held a stretcher on which was huddled Harry Rogan. One of the men held Harry's hand. Lucy heard Harry moaning—good, he was still alive. There was blood everywhere, seeping from under a red pad that one man held over Harry's chest and arm. There was a puddle of blood on the truck floor, a pool of it in the stretcher.

'Bring him out gently,' Lucy said. 'Take him straight into the office and put him on the couch. Keep that pad pressed tight, I'll get you another one inside.'

The men did as she told them. Lucy took a large

pair of scissors from the cabinet, began to cut away
Harry's clothes, sodden with both water and blood.
She leaned over and whispered into Harry's mud-
caked ear. 'It's going to be all right, Harry, we've got
everything under control.' She repressed the bit of her
mind that screamed that this was none of her business.
From the cabinet she took two space blankets,
wrapped them round the now nearly naked body.
Harry would be going into shock.

Something appeared in her memory, from a book
or television programme. Take a complete case history. 'Exactly what happened?' she asked.

'He was trimming a branch off a felled tree. The
tree slipped and pushed the saw back onto his chest.
We scratched the earth away from under him and
dragged him out.'

'So it's only his chest that's injured?' Only his
chest?

The small room was full, too full of anxious men.
'Go and help yourself to coffee,' Lucy ordered. 'If
we need you we'll shout.'

'He's going to be all right?' one of the men asked.

'We're in touch with head office. They're sending
out a doctor by chopper.' The men filed out.

'They're not sending a doctor,' Jerry whispered
tautly behind her. 'There's one standing by all right,
but there's no way it could get through this weather.
It's going to be a few hours before it will be safe to
land.'

'We can't cope with this on our own, we need
help.'

There was a sound from the radio behind them.
Jerry listened, then said, 'It's the big boss, Royston

himself. He wants to talk to you.' He handed the headset to her.

'How's my brother?' a voice asked. It was calm, but she thought she could sense the tension underneath.

'He's alive but he's lost an awful lot of blood. There's a massive cut across the top of his chest and shoulder. Airways, breathing and circulation appear to be okay. There's a cabinet full of stuff here and I just don't know what to do with it.'

'I'm patching you through to a doctor who'll stay on air and direct you—she knows what's in the cabinet, you just do as she tells you. Lucy—it is Lucy, isn't it?—are you up to doing this?'

'Yes, it is Lucy, and I'll do the best I can. I won't faint or anything.'

'Good. Dr Ballard is here.'

Another calm voice on the line—a female one. 'Hi, Lucy, my name's Annie and together we're going to see to this poor young man. This is the golden hour, treatment now can save his life. We can do it, Lucy. Just hold onto that and we'll do fine.'

Tartly, Lucy said, 'You can stop boosting my confidence and we'll start on what needs to be done.'

She heard a chuckle. 'Right on. Now how long and how deep is the cut, and has the bleeding stopped?'

Annie was a good guide. She might have been miles away but at the time Lucy felt she was by her side. Following instructions, she snapped on rubber gloves. She had kept up the pressure on the pad over the dreadful cut, and now it seemed the flow of blood was stopping. So the first essential was somehow to replace the vast quantity of blood Harry had lost. 'We need intravenous access,' Annie said. 'This means you're going to have to stick a special hollow needle into a vein in his arm. Now, can you see a thick blue line on the inside of Harry's arm, opposite his elbow?'

Following instructions, Lucy swabbed the area of skin, forced in the thick needle—not too deeply, Annie warned—connected the needle to what was called a giving set, and saw the first trickle of plasma drip into Harry's vein. Jerry was behind her, fetching what she needed from the cabinet. Annie told Lucy how to carry out simple tests—check pulse, breathing, even blood pressure with an electronic machine. She scattered an antiseptic powder over the wound, and kept it covered with sterile dressings. She fixed an oxygen mask to Harry's face, and turned it on.

Because Annie's voice was constantly with her, Lucy didn't stop to think what she was doing. Tasks that an hour ago she would have thought far beyond her, she now performed. Not easily, but she did them. Finally, there was nothing more to do.

'We wait now,' Annie said. 'Keep up the observations and let me know if anything at all changes.'

'You're not disappearing?' Lucy protested.

'Certainly not. I'm on this line with you till Harry's shipped out in the chopper. Incidentally, how long since you had a drink, Lucy?'

What an odd question. 'It seems hours,' Lucy said, 'but I'm not hungry or...'

'Get someone to fetch you a coffee. And eat a bar of chocolate or something. And don't tell me you don't feel like it.'

Lucy had now got into the habit of doing everything Annie told her. She asked Jerry to fetch her the chocolate and coffee. Then she looked anxiously at

Harry. The man who was—she now realised—her patient.

'Annie, there's something a bit queer about his breathing. He seems to be panting, as if he can't get enough air. And he seems to be less conscious than before.'

'Feel his jugular vein on the side of his neck. Is there a pulse there? Is the vein raised?'

When Lucy looked, she saw what Annie meant. 'Yes. And I don't think it was there before.'

'And you said that there's injury to one side of the chest only.' For the first time Lucy thought she detected the sounds of strain in Annie's voice, and she realised how impotent the doctor must be feeling. But her instructions were as clear as ever.

'I think Harry's got what we call a tension pneumothorax. Air is leaking out of his lung into the cavity surrounding it, and stopping the lung working. It'll collapse in time.'

'So what do I...?'

'You'll have to push a tube into the space outside the lung and let the air out. The important thing is to make sure you get the hole in the right place. Now, you're going to need a sixteen g cannula, they're in the cabinet...'

Jerry came back then with her coffee and chocolate, and she told him to break off half the chocolate and put it straight into her mouth. Then she followed Annie's detailed instructions, found the right place on the chest, forced in the needle of the syringe. There was the hoped-for release of air. Then she slid the cannula down the needle into what she now knew was the pleural cavity, and fixed it in place with strapping.

'Breathing's better,' she reported back to Annie, 'and he seems less distressed.'

'Good. You sound like a girl with a mouth half full of chocolate.'

'I feel better for it,' Lucy confessed. 'I hadn't realised just how stressed I was getting.'

'So drink some coffee now. With any luck all we have to do further is wait. When you've had your coffee you can go through the routine observations again.'

Harry seemed to be holding his own. The blood flow stopped after a while, and she changed the bottle dropping plasma into his arm. If anything, waiting was worse than actually working from Annie's instructions. She was responsible for everything that had been done to Harry, but what if she had done something wrong? Then another voice came through the radio. 'Lucy, we think there's a window in the weather. Tell Jerry that the chopper should be landing in fifteen minutes, there's a medical team on board and they'll move Harry straight out. In fact, put Jerry on for a minute.'

'Right,' said Lucy, and reached for the rest of her chocolate.

She had one last word with Annie. 'Whatever you do, don't try to work now,' Annie said. 'You're to take yourself to bed, keep warm, try to sleep for a couple of hours.'

'But I've got to cook…'

'Doctor's orders, Lucy. Let them cook for themselves.'

Even as Annie spoke, Lucy heard a distant hum that rapidly turned into the thunder of engines. She looked out of the window—the first time for hours!—

and saw men sprinting towards her, heads bent to avoid the still whirling rotor blades. Jerry opened the door. 'I'm Dr Wentworth,' a voice said. 'Now what have you got for us?'

In its way, the view from the skyscraper window was nearly as impressive as the view from the cookhouse in camp. Downtown Seattle spread below her, and she could see the space needle, the monorail, the ships crossing Elliot Bay. She remembered that Royston Rogan had interests in shipping as well as logging.

Apart from the view, the office itself didn't seem too much out of the ordinary. The desk was cluttered, there was a golf bag leaning against the filing cabinet, and articles cut from newspapers had been stuck to the walls with tape. Definitely an office for working in.

It had been a full week since Harry's accident. Dr Wentworth had listened to her account of what she had done as he had performed a swift, but what she had recognised as a far more proficient, examination. 'Annie Ballard is good,' he had said absently. 'I wouldn't want to treat someone over the radio. Now I think we're ready to move Harry out of here. Good work, Lucy.' And the team, Harry and chopper were gone.

She wondered what she was feeling as she watched the giant machine dwindle into the sky. Then she realised. She wanted to burst into tears. Gruffly, Jerry said, 'Boss's orders, Lucy. You're to go to bed, stay there till tomorrow morning. We'll make our own dinner.'

'You certainly will not! There's nothing wrong with me, I just feel...'

But Royston Rogan had spoken, and what he said was law. In fact, to her amazement she did sleep. She only woke when Jerry tapped on her door, with coffee, a steak sandwich, and some more than welcome news. 'Just heard on the radio. They got Harry to the hospital in time, he's going to make it.'

Next morning she felt fine, woke at the usual early hour and went to start the breakfasts. Life would go on as before. But then came a summons—Lucy was to go to Seattle for a week, a helicopter would come to pick her up, and bring in a relief cook. And here she was.

She felt a little out of place in her boots, jeans and red plaid shirt. As she'd been escorted across the lobby below she'd been surrounded by dozens of beautifully groomed secretaries. In this building, everybody power-dressed. Perhaps she should have put a dress on; there was one in the camouflage rucksack by her feet. It held all her worldly possessions—well, all those she had in America.

The office door slammed open. 'Lucy Brett? I'm Royston Rogan, call me Roy. First of all, thanks for everything you did for my brother. Sit down and we'll have some coffee.' He had brought a tray in with him.

Lucy took the outstretched hand. Royston Rogan wasn't at all what she had expected. He was young— she guessed not more than about twelve years older than herself. He wasn't a tall man—about five foot nine, a couple of inches taller than she was. But he radiated energy. He talked quickly, walking round the room as if he couldn't bear to keep still.

'I brought you down here to thank you myself. And because I wanted to see what kind of person saved my brother's life. You know you did save his life, don't you?'

'Dr Ballard really did it,' Lucy said cautiously. 'I only followed her instructions.'

'I've talked to Annie, and I've talked to Dr Wentworth. I know what you did, so I want less of the British sense of reserve. You did a great job, Lucy, and I'm going to thank you. The question is how.'

'I like Harry and I was pleased to help him,' Lucy said. 'Any of the men would have done what I did, it just sort of fell to me.'

'Just sort of fell. That's one way of putting it. Anyway, I've got a proposition for you. I gather you have no medical training whatsoever?'

'Not a bit,' she said cheerfully.

'Did you enjoy working on Harry?'

'Not enjoy, I was terrified. And since then I've thought I'd like to learn a bit more—I don't want to be stuck feeling so helpless again.'

'Perfect! Lucy, there's a three-month intensive course for paramedics, run at the university here. Just the course that Pete Lynch went on. If you want to go on it, I'll pay the fees and your salary while you're there. Then you're back in the woods, but not as a cook.'

This was just what she wanted! She hadn't realised it until Roy had asked her—but now she knew there was nothing she'd rather do. But... 'Just one thing,' she said. 'I tend to be a bit of a wanderer. How long would you expect me to stay with you if you paid for the course?'

'Twelve months minimum,' he said. 'But I hope you'll stay longer. Quite frankly, Lucy, you're the kind of person I'm looking for. I can see you going far in my organisation.'

She thought a moment. Then, 'Done,' she said.

'Good. The course starts in ten days, you can liaise with my secretary who will find you somewhere to live and organise all the details.' He paused, and she almost thought he seemed embarrassed. This couldn't be—she'd never seen a more self-confident man.

'One more thing, Lucy. And this you can certainly refuse if you wish, I don't blackmail my staff. Tomorrow night there's a big charity bash in the city. You know, black tie, dinner, dancing, all in a good cause. Will you come as my partner?'

'I thought you were married,' she said cautiously.

She saw the pain flit across his face. 'I am. My wife had a horse-riding accident, hit her head. She's alive, but in a coma, and the doctors say she will never come out of it. They call it PVS. Persistent Vegetative State.'

'I'd love to come with you as your partner,' Lucy said softly, 'but as you can see—' she pointed to her jeans '—I really don't have anything to wear.'

'Another secretary problem,' Roy said. 'She can take you out, buy you a dress on the firm. She'll enjoy that.' He walked over to the door, opened it and shouted, 'Millie, have you got a minute…?'

'Miss Tremblett is waiting to see you,' the unseen secretary's voice said.

Before Roy could say anything a woman entered the room, presumably Miss Tremblett. Lucy surveyed her with interest. Miss Tremblett had spent more on her hair than Lucy had on her entire outfit, including everything in the rucksack. The blue silk shirt, the grey silk suit, the high, high heels—they had cost a fortune. Roy promptly introduced the two, and Lucy accepted a frigidly extended kid-gloved hand.

Miss Tremblett looked at Lucy with equal interest—not to say disdain. 'You must be the little girl that helped Roy's brother,' she said.

Right, thought Lucy, I'll have you. 'I did my little best,' she said.

Roy sensed trouble. 'I've got things I have to discuss with Miss Tremblett,' he said to Lucy. 'Why don't I hand you over to Millie and she can take you shopping? Can we meet for lunch?'

'I'd like that,' Lucy said. 'So nice meeting you, Miss Tremblett.'

The hotel room Roy had booked for Lucy was vastly different from the wood and tin cabin she inhabited in the logging camp. And though she loved the life out there, she had to admit that a bit of unadulterated luxury every now and again was most enjoyable. In the camp she showered in an outhouse. Here there was a vast circular bath, and she had luxuriated in foam up to her chin.

She had just had a wonderful, essentially feminine day. Apparently Roy had given Millie, his secretary, quite detailed instructions. Every time Lucy had expressed doubt about the amount of money they were spending, Millie had said, 'But it's what Mr Roy ordered.' Yesterday they had bought shoes, clothes; today they had visited an expensive hairdresser's and beautician's. The manicurist had looked at Lucy's nails, and shuddered visibly. 'Would Madam like artificial nails, perhaps?' she had asked.

'Madam would not,' Lucy had answered cheerfully.

But they had done a good job. As she sat in front of her mirror, Lucy could hardly recognise herself. Millie had started from her underwear and worked outwards. Gone were the sensible garments that were just the thing for the camp—instead she had a white lacy half-bra with matching briefs. Sheer stockings— stay-ups, not tights. High-heeled strappy shoes in a shade of blue that complemented the darker blue of her silk dress.

Usually she wore her dark hair medium long, drawn back with a bow to hold it. The hairdresser had cut it, shaped it, blown it so it curled round her face, and accentuated her dark grey eyes. 'You look good, Brett,' she said out loud. 'Now let's go to the party.'

Roy was picking her up in five minutes.

She was glad he didn't call for her in a stretch limousine. Her sense of humour would have got the better of her. Instead there was a large silver Mercedes, chauffeur driven, of course.

'Lucy, you look stunning,' he said, his eyes frankly admiring. 'What happened to the tomboy I offered a job to?'

'Still me,' she said airily. 'I hope the food at this do is as good as I cook.'

'If it isn't, please don't tell the chef,' he begged her. 'We've flown him in from San Francisco.'

'I shall observe like a fellow professional. Will we be at the same table as Miss Tremblett?'

'We will. It was all arranged weeks ago. Lucy, you are going to behave yourself, aren't you?'

'Oh, yes,' she said, 'I shall conduct myself like a real lady.'

The Mercedes drew up outside a grand hotel, where there was a canopy to the front doors and a red carpet stretching across the pavement. A footman opened the car door and Roy offered her his arm.

They walked across the glittering foyer, and waited in a short queue as the guests in front of them were announced by a loud-voiced Master of Ceremonies. 'Mr and Mrs James Detterling...Miss Darlene Kells and Mr Charles Noble...Mr and Mrs Leonard Trent and their daughter Maria.'

Now it was their turn. Lucy could see the great room in front of them, see the already assembled guests watching the new arrivals. Roy handed the MC the card with their names on. The MC looked up, and Roy gave him a peremptory nod.

'Lady Lucy Brett,' bellowed the MC, 'and Mr Royston Rogan.' Lucy and Roy walked over to their table.

Miss Tremblett was not best pleased. 'What was that nonsense about Lady Brett?' she asked angrily. 'You're not a...'

'I hope you're not going to say that I'm not a lady,' Lucy said cheerfully, 'because I most certainly am. Roy here didn't believe me either, so I got him to phone my father, Lord Brett.'

'Quite true.' Roy grinned. 'He had to phone me back from the House of Lords.'

'The title was given us in 1675, by Charles the Second,' Lucy went on, 'just about seventy years after Virginia was first colonised.'

Roy decided this was enough. 'There's someone over here I want you to meet,' he said, pulling a sweetly smiling Lucy away. 'We'll be back shortly.'

'Did I say something wrong?' Lucy asked, mock innocently.

'Now I know how you managed to pull my brother

through. You don't back away from anything, do you? If a fight is offered, then you'll go for it.'

'She tried to patronise me,' Lucy said. 'So I did the same back to her.'

'I think you're going to be an asset to my company,' he said, 'and I'd like to see more of you.'

'I enjoy working for your company and we can be friends. But that's all, Roy. While you have a wife, that's all we can ever be.'

'Now how did I know you were going to say that? Come on, let's meet a few people.'

The intensive three-month paramedic course was hard work. But Lucy was used to that. In fact she often felt frustrated—there was more that she wanted to know but there just wasn't time to study it. They were trained as paramedics specifically for the logging camps, so whole areas of expertise were left out. There was no dealing with children, no dealing with problems of childbirth. But she learned.

Four or five times Roy took her out to dinner. She liked his company but she made sure he stuck to the rules she had set. 'No one's going to snigger about us, Roy, I won't have it.' After the first couple of meetings, he realised she meant what she said, and took her out just for the pleasure of being with her.

Then the course was over, and she was sent out to a logging camp. Lucy was pleased that he didn't try to find her an easy job; the camp was perched on a mountainside in some of the most desolate country imaginable. She enjoyed the work, the challenge. After she had climbed a rock face to splint the leg of a logger who had fallen, the men accepted her. She was happy.

Whenever she had a break from her duties she came back to Seattle, and Roy always took her out. 'What's your story, Lucy?' he asked once. 'How come that you, a lady in your own right, and a very bright girl too, ends up bumming round America?'

By now Roy was a trusted friend. She gave him an honest answer. 'I'm looking for something,' she told him.

'And you don't know what it is?'

'Exactly right.'

Then one day she found what she was looking for. There were still a few native Americans to be found in the forests. Mostly they didn't lead the noble life of the Red Indian of myth, but lived in drunken squalor. And one evening a woman came into the camp and asked if anyone could help her baby. She was very sick.

Lucy took some food and a box with what medical supplies she thought might be of use. But she had no idea how to diagnose, how to treat a three-year-old child. She did what she could to make the child comfortable, and went back to camp to send an urgent radio message to the nearest doctor. Next day she learned the child had died.

'In a month I will have finished the year I promised you,' she told Roy at their next meeting. 'I've enjoyed the work, and I thank you for training me. But now I know what I want to do with my life. I'm going back to England to train to be a doctor.'

'Why go back to England? We have good hospitals here. If you want I will sponsor you, I know I'll get my money's worth out of you.'

She shook her head. 'It's time I went home, Roy.

Now that I know what I want, it's time to rejoin my family.'

By now he knew better than to try to persuade her to change her mind. 'I'll miss you, Lucy. You will keep in touch?'

'I'll keep in touch,' she promised.

CHAPTER ONE

MEDICINE? thought Gray Woods. Is this medicine?

I have studied, learned and trained for thirteen years, since I was eighteen. I am now a specialist registrar in Paediatric Oncology, known and re-spected—I hope and think—by my colleagues. Papers I have written have been published in medical and scientific journals. Doctors come to listen to me when I lecture. So what am I doing here?

A breeze blew across the playing field, and he shiv-ered. 'It's cold, isn't it?' he asked the man sitting next to him.

The man blinked. 'Well, I would have said it was quite warm for October,' he said. 'Of course, if you're not used to British weather...'

Gray thought back bitterly to a fortnight ago. He had been thousands of miles away, playing beach ten-nis. Every fifteen minutes, both teams had dashed into the sea to cool off, it had been fun. Not like this.

'Your turn, Dr Woods,' the attendant said with a happy smile. 'No one's managed it yet, good luck.'

Gray stood, and tried to work up some enthusiasm. Once he had been an international class athlete, so what was this but a different form of athletics? Where was his sense of humour? Perhaps he was still jet-lagged.

He was wearing a tall pink hat, and had a matching pink false nose tied onto his face. Thick braces held a hoop round his middle, and from it hung pink and white striped trousers. It looked as if he had a sixty-inch waist. It wasn't the most elegant he had ever looked.

He was helped up a ladder onto a narrow plank, where five feet below him was a tub filled with re-volting-looking green gunge. Somewhere a bell sounded, and there was a roar of applause. Arms spread wide, he started to inch his way along the plank. Suddenly it hit him, that combination of ner-vousness and exhilaration that he had used to feel immediately before a race. No one yet had managed to get to the other side. But he was going to!

The opposing team was all female, dressed as elves, in pointy hats, false ears and skimpy costumes. Most seemed to have been soaked in some earlier game, for their costumes were stuck to them. They seemed attractive girls, he thought, probably nurses.

The elves' job was to stop him, knock him off the plank into the gunge by throwing great balls of foam at him. He thought that, although large, the balls would be of negligible weight. But then the first one hit him, and to a roar from the crowd he nearly fell in. Waving his arms frantically, he managed to get back his balance. The foam balls were heavier than he had thought.

Now he knew what to expect. The next two balls he managed to duck, the third he saw coming and deliberately leaned into, knocking it down onto the gunge below. Then he teetered a few more steps. He was getting the idea; his reflexes were as good as ever. He dodged or pushed away a further three balls.

He was nearer the elves now, their aim was better and the balls hit him with more force. Making pro-gress was getting harder. But he was going to make

it. The determination that once made him a top athlete
was surfacing again. He remembered the words of his
old coach—if you're not going out there to win, why
bother going out there at all?

The little platform that was his goal was now quite
close. The elves were throwing at almost point-blank
range, and the balls hurt. He ducked one, turned side-
ways to keep his balance, then twisted to run the last
three steps that would lead him to safety. And there
facing him was a very wet elf. She was standing on
the plank in front of him, arms raised, holding a ball
over her head. Surely this was against the rules?

A tiny part of his mind registered how attractive
the elf was. She was taller than average, with long,
long legs; her breasts were clearly outlined against
the stretched wet fabric of her shirt. And she was
laughing at him! He tried to shout that this wasn't
fair, when the ball hit him in the chest. He slipped,
teetered again, and fell head first into the green gunge
below.

It was as cold, wet, sticky and disgusting as it
looked.

He surfaced, climbed to his feet and saw the elf
above him, pointing and laughing. She thinks she is
far out of reach, he thought. Out of reach of a normal
man, but he'd been an athlete who could jump.

He crouched, leaped, one hand caught the plank
and the other reached for her ankle. He caught the
ankle, twisted. It was some distance for her to fall,
and he didn't want her to get hurt so he contrived to
get underneath her. With a tremendous splat they fell
into the gunge together.

They both knelt up together, and he helped her to
her feet. They were both covered with green. He

couldn't help himself—he pulled her sticky face to him and kissed her. The two of them stared at each other, speechless.

There was a cheer from the crowd, and the flash of cameras. He lifted his arms up, as he had used to do when he had won a race. Then he felt her foot hook behind his ankle and pull forward. He fell back into the gunge again. Then there was the same foot on his chest, pushing him down. This little elf liked winning just as much as he did!

He did manage to struggle to his feet, and in fact the elf helped him. 'Are you all right?' she asked sweetly. 'Not swallowed too much? Shall I send for a stomach pump?'

'If you're the nurse that's going to operate it, then no, thanks. Anyway, wasn't it against the rules for you to be on that plank?'

'Probably,' she said, without much apparent guilt. 'But you did a lovely fall, and it's all in aid of charity. You didn't really mind, did you?'

'Not really. Not if you didn't mind my kissing you.'

'I didn't mind at all, it was all in aid of charity.' He wondered what she'd look like if she weren't dressed as a wet elf.

Her friends were calling her now. 'Come on, Lucy, we've got to go over to living chess.' She turned to struggle out of the tank. A voice called him, too. 'You did best of all on the plank, Dr Woods. But now you're wanted for the back of the elephant.' He would have liked another couple of words with the elf, but she had gone.

The rest of the afternoon was equally full. After being the hind legs of an elephant that had to run an obstacle course, he played another three games. He enjoyed himself, for some of the tasks he was given needed surprising skill. He jousted with a rubber spear, tried to stay on top of a giant ball, wriggled through plastic tunnels. Competing again was fun—he'd forgotten the adrenaline rush.

For most of the time his mind was firmly fixed on the games, but he was aware of lots of spectators, of press and TV photographers. The charity should be making plenty of money, and he was glad, for it was the aim of the afternoon.

He didn't see the elves again.

By the end of the afternoon he was weary. He trudged back to the communal changing rooms. Outside he met Melissa Yates, the neurology registrar who had talked him into taking part.

'Gray, you did so well,' she told him. 'I was watching you—it was easy to see you were a trained athlete.'

'There's no training to fit you to be the back of an elephant,' he told her. 'I've got aches where I didn't know I had muscles.'

'You'll feel better after a hot shower. Now I've got to spend an hour or so with the organisers, but we think we've done rather well, made plenty of money. Afterwards a group of us are meeting in the doctors' lounge for a bit of a party—you'll come, won't you?'

'I'd love to but...' A vast weariness fell on him. He knew what it was, of course: jet lag. If he did go to the party he'd only fall asleep. 'It's only three days since I arrived from Australia,' he said ruefully, 'and I'm feeling the strain a bit. I guess I'd better just go to bed.'

'And you said you're on call tomorrow. D'you

want me to phone your consultant? See if you can have tomorrow morning off?'

'Never! I'm here to work. Seriously, Melissa, I'll be all right, I'll just take a taxi home.'

He had a quick shower in the changing rooms, then took a taxi back to the hospital and treated himself to a long, relaxing bath. It was Saturday night, so not a lot of people were staying in. He made himself a cheese sandwich, a large mug of cocoa and went back to his room. Once there he poured a large tot of duty-free brandy into the cocoa. That should help him sleep!

But, of course, he didn't sleep. He was jet-lagged, typically he felt weary, but couldn't sleep. He lay on his bed and thought about the last couple of days. So much had happened, so much to remember.

His room here in the hospital was fine. He liked living on top of the job, and, since he was only here for six months, there was no point in looking for a flat. He knew he was going to enjoy the work—Lizzie's was famous as a paediatric hospital, and the oncology consultant, his immediate boss Adam Harrison, had an international reputation. Gray was here to work and learn, and he knew he'd learn a lot from Adam. For a while he thought about the next six months, questions he wanted answering, research projects he needed to check.

And he'd enjoyed today. Once he'd got used to the cold, it had been fine. It was just that first game—when he'd been knocked into the green gunge by that elf. Perhaps she had bent the rules a little but he saw something of himself in her. A determination to get things done. And she had been so attractive—he thought. He frowned. He was here for six months, to

learn and work. No time for frivolous diversions.
Such as elves? a voice in his brain asked. He drained
his mug of cocoa, and reached up to put out the light.

He wasn't on duty, but he was on call. And next
morning he was called over to the ward.

'John Ryan, get back in your bed or I will come
down this ward and trimbouliate you! And the same
goes for the rest of your little gang!'

It was a female voice that could have been pleasant.
But at the moment it was loud and stern and it clearly
meant what it said. There was silence at first in
Swallow Ward, and then the scurry of feet.

Outside the ward Gray looked at ward sister Lisa
Fletcher. 'Who was that?' he asked. 'And what does
trimbouliate mean?'

Lisa looked up at him blandly. 'That is one of our
two senior house officers, Dr Lucy Brett. You may
make up your own mind about how good she is med-
ically. But she's the best disciplinarian we've ever
had on the ward. And if trimbouliation keeps the kids
as quiet as she does, then I'm all in favour of it.'

Gray nodded. Paediatric wards took children of all
ages up to sixteen. Sometimes controlling the older
children could be a problem. They were bored, they
often didn't feel ill, they just naturally got into mis-
chief. And when there was more than one of them...if
she could deal with this, then this doctor deserved
respect. 'Dr Brett just phoned me,' he said. 'She's a
bit concerned about a Mary Peterson.'

Lisa looked grave. 'We're all concerned. D'you
want me to come down and look at her with you?'

He shook his head. 'I'm feeling my way here. I'd
like to have a word with Dr Brett first.' He pushed

open the ward door, and saw a tallish female figure.
She had her back to him, and he saw dark trousers
that emphasised long legs, with the bright coloured
tabard that so many doctors and nurses wore on paediatric wards. Her hair was dark, cut short.

'Dr Brett?' She turned. He had a swift impression
of enormous grey eyes, with a cheerful smile. She was
perhaps a bit older than the other SHO whom he'd
met two days before, who looked more like a school-
boy than a doctor. She wasn't dressed as an elf any
more, but he recognised her at once. This was the girl
who had knocked him into the green gunge, the girl
he had dragged in, the girl he had kissed. His SHO!

She recognised him at once too. He saw her initial
shock, and then an impudent smile. 'Oh, dear! Did I
push my specialist registrar into the evil green
gunge—and when he was doing so well? You'll have
to report me to the BMA!'

Since Gray wanted to talk before examining Mary,
Lucy took him into the doctors' room. The desk at
which she sat to do her interminable paperwork was
already piled high. But that was for later. She poured
two cups of the inevitable coffee. They sat at each
side of the coffee-table and looked at each other with
undisguised curiosity.

Now he was no longer dressed as a clown she saw
that he was a…well, a personable man. He was wearing fawn trousers, with a white shirt, and she was glad
he didn't look too formal. Not a good idea on a children's ward. His body looked very trim, athletic
even—she remembered how he had leaped up to grab
her ankle, when she wouldn't have thought it possible. His bronzed face was interesting rather than con-

ventionally handsome, though there was a touch of sternness, almost bleakness about his eyes and lips. She felt he wouldn't be a good man to cross. But his smile seemed friendly enough.

She would offer him an olive branch. 'I hope I did no serious damage throwing you into the pool,' she said. 'I know I probably cheated, but…'

'The spectators liked it, so why not? That was the aim of the exercise.'

She liked this, and felt it was the right attitude. 'I've been in touch with the organisers. We did well,' she told him. 'We—and you helped—made a lot of money for the hospital charity.'

'Ask me to help again,' he told her.

Then he said nothing more. She found the silence, the level gaze, rather disturbing. She wanted to tell him more about the money they had raised, but didn't quite know how to do it. So she decided to stick to the matter in hand.

'I phoned you, Dr Woods,' she started, 'because…'

He interrupted her. 'Call me Gray, short for Graham. I thought you pommies had stopped being so formal.'

This was good. 'We have…Gray,' she told him. 'It's just that some doctors—especially from overseas—tend to be, well, dinosaurs. I'm glad to know you're one of us. I'm Lucy, by the way, and, though I get it, I don't like Luce.' She offered her hand.

He took it solemnly. 'I'll remember that. And if I call you Luce, Lucy, you'll know I'm mad at you.'

He looked down at their hands, still joined, and let go of her, quickly. Touching her seemed to have affected him, reminding him of something. So far she had found him very friendly, this man who had kissed her, but now he seemed to shut down, and his voice became curt. 'What's wrong with this Mary Peterson?'

Lucy wasn't going to take bad temper from anyone on the staff, senior or otherwise, if she hadn't deserved it. 'We'll go and see in a minute,' she said, saccharin sweet, 'but are you okay? I gather you only came from Australia a few days ago—you must be very tired.'

He shook his head, and she knew he had caught the falseness of her concern. But when he spoke, she knew he had forgiven her.

'Probably I am still jet-lagged, but I don't feel it. I'm having difficulty in getting used to things—the weather, for a start. But I'm looking forward to being here, and I'm hoping to learn a lot.'

'I like people with ambition,' she told him honestly. 'I'm ambitious myself.'

She felt him looking at her, perhaps reassessing her. 'Why did you pick Oncology?' he asked. 'Cancer is a tough speciality.'

'I hope you're not suggesting that it's not suitable for women. I hope you don't mean that we're not capable of facing up to it?'

'Not at all. I've worked with some brilliant female oncologists at home.'

She paused, then, 'Sorry,' she said. 'I get a bit paranoid at times about what women are and are not capable of. Cancer interests me because…I think we're making constant progress. A lot of people don't know just how far we've come in the past thirty years, the number who survive now who would have died then. Well, I anticipate similar changes and I want to be part of them. And who knows?' She shrugged. 'Perhaps we'll get the big breakthrough on lung or breast or prostate cancer.'

'And why paediatric cancer? Why children?'

The answer to that was simple. 'Of all childhood diseases up to the age of fourteen, the biggest killer is cancer.'

'That's a good answer, I like it.'

He paused. She thought he was going to question her more closely about her thoughts and ideas. Surprisingly, she would have liked him to. For some reason, she wanted this man to know how she felt. But he returned to the matter in hand.

'Tell me about Mary Peterson. Then we'll go and have a look. Are her parents there?'

'They'll be along presently,' Lucy said. 'They're a devoted pair, at least one of them visits every day. Right now they're both in church.'

'You know that for certain?'

'Know the parents, know the child,' Lucy recited. 'Adam Harrison, our consultant, he always says that.'

'I'll say it myself in future, it's very wise. Now, Mary?'

Lucy marshalled her facts, separated her feelings from the bare essentials. 'Mary Peterson, three years three months old. An only child. She presented with stage one Wilms' tumour—nephroblastoma.' This meant that Mary had a tumour on her kidney, but stage one meant that it had been caught very early. 'We were very lucky to catch it so soon, she had a very good GP who spotted it. Anyway, we had the kidney excised, and followed with radiotherapy and chemotherapy. But Mary's vital signs are down. I wonder if we ought to—moderate the chemotherapy?' She detailed the drugs prescribed by the consultant.

He was testing her. 'What's the success rate for treatment of Wilms' tumour?'

'About eighty per cent. Which is still twenty per cent short of what we need.'

'Good. Now you know we always have to keep a balance between cytotoxic drugs and the health of the patient. We'll have a look at Mary and see if we can ease up a bit on her prescription.'

Lucy knew that cytotoxic drugs actually killed cells, but that they were used with success to combat cancer. But they were never pleasant in their effect.

She collected Lisa and took Gray to Mary's bedside. There she noticed how Gray took the listless little girl's hand, and talked to her for a while before carrying on with his examination.

'How has she been, Lisa?' he asked the ward sister.

Lucy liked that. She felt that the nursing staff often had a lot of valuable observations to make, and that too many doctors ignored this fact.

Lisa hesitated, then said, 'By now, other children of the same age and with the same drugs are usually doing better than Mary.'

'Yes, I would have thought so.' He pondered a minute, then said, 'We'll maintain the dosage, at least until tonight. Keep an eye on her, and if there's the least change in her condition, I want to know about it.'

He went back to Mary's bedside, settled the teddy beside her and straightened her bedclothes.

'What are you doing now?' he asked Lucy.

'Nothing very much,' she said airily. 'I've got the bloods and the To Take Out forms and the drug reports. Not to mention keeping a close eye on our fifteen-year-old gangsters.'

'An easy day, in fact. Would you like to wander round the ward with me for five minutes, tell me about anyone you find interesting?'

She thought it was an unusual request. 'All right,' she said. 'Not a proper ward round, just a getting-to-know-you exercise?'

'Exactly. I can tell it's the weekend, there's plenty of visitors around.'

As much as was possible, Lizzie's had an open-ward policy. Parents were encouraged to spend as much time as they could with their children. For most little patients this was fine, but there were children who, for various reasons, rarely had a visitor. Then it was up to the nursing staff to try to provide the tender loving care that every child needed.

They wandered down the ward, peering in the four-bedded bays and the little side rooms. Some bays were largely silent, with perhaps a couple of parents sitting by a motionless child's bed. Other bays were lively, noisy even as the patients tried the new games their parents had brought in.

'Do you have open wards in Australia?' she asked him. 'Parents can cause a bit of havoc at times—but having them here is really good for the children.'

He didn't answer at once, but stood watching. A six-year-old with a completely shaven head sat entranced as his mother, sitting on the bed beside him, showed him how to work a GameBoy. Then, 'The hospital I worked in is responsible for the paediatric care of a great section of the outback. They get cases from stations seven or eight hundred miles away. Quite often the parents just can't get in to see their children. The children need our specialised care but they miss out on love.'

'It's a problem all children's hospitals have. But it must be worse with those distances involved.'

'We started a pilot scheme just as I left, called Granny for an Hour. Local people who had enough time were invited to come in whenever they could, almost adopt a child for a while. There were difficulties, of course, screening the volunteers was bad enough. But in general it worked. The children benefited. Usually the parents were very grateful. And I think the volunteers got a lot out of it too.'

'Whose idea was that?' she asked, suspecting from his enthusiasm that she knew the answer.

He turned to grin at her. 'Mine. And I'm proud of it.'

They turned into a bay with only one person inside. The other three boys from the bay now had their parents visiting; they were probably all sitting in the day room. But one solitary figure sat on his bed, indicating by the intent way he was studying his magazine that he didn't care whether he had a visitor or not.

'Hello, John,' Lucy said cheerfully. 'This is a new doctor, Dr Woods. Gray, this is John Ryan.'

'Didn't hear you there,' John lied valiantly. 'Hi, Doc, how's it going?'

'Doctor, not Doc,' Lucy corrected. 'What are you reading, John?'

Sheepishly John showed them the article. 'It's about cooking vegetables,' he said. 'I thought I'd like to train to be a cook. When I get out of this place.'

'I used to be a cook in America,' she told him. 'When I get time I'll bring you some photographs showing you where I worked. And the books they gave me to work from.'

'Thanks, Lucy. See you, Doc...Doctor.'

'He looks fit,' Gray said as they walked away. 'What's his prognosis?'

'He's been in and out of here for years. He has AML—acute myeloblastic leukaemia. At the moment he's in remission, and if he had a good home to go to he'd probably be sent there. But he hasn't. No mother, a father who has two other children and doesn't care too much anyway.'

'Hmm. AML and a poor home life. Not much of a prospect. Could we arrange for him to be shown round the hospital kitchens? Perhaps have a word with the head cook?'

She looked at him in surprise. 'That's a really good idea,' she said. 'And it's so obvious, why didn't I think of it?'

'Perhaps you were happy trimbouliating him,' Gray said, straight-faced.

'Trimbouliating! Oh! You must have heard me earlier through the ward door. I'm sorry, I was just…'

'Don't worry. I think that every doctor should be able to prescribe a touch of trimbouliation from time to time.'

They were now back at the entrance to the ward. He put his hand on her shoulder, and for some reason she shivered at his gentle touch. 'Well, thanks for showing me round, Lucy,' he said. 'I think I'd better leave you to your paperwork now. I'm looking forward to our working together. Don't forget, even the slightest doubt about Mary, bleep me.' He turned to go, then, 'Some time, will you tell me about when you were a cook?' he asked.

'Some time, perhaps. But that was in another life. I'm a doctor now.'

'Good.' And he was gone.

There was a delicate cough, and Lucy turned to see Lisa beckoning her to come into the sister's room. It was obviously time for a gossip. 'What d'you think of him?' Lisa asked when the two of them were shut in together.

'A bit reserved,' Lucy said. 'I thought all Australians were supposed to be outgoing and shout "Good on yer, sport" at every opportunity.'

'I like him,' Lisa said. 'I think he's gorgeous.'

Yes, Lucy thought with some surprise, he is gorgeous. 'He kissed me yesterday,' she said, 'after I pushed him into a tank full of green stuff.'

'Brett, you pick the strangest way of attracting men.'

Did she want to attract Gray Woods?

CHAPTER TWO

LUCY needed a rest and for once there was no one in the doctors' room. She slumped into the armchair, kicked off her shoes and lifted her feet onto the coffee-table. Then she closed her eyes. In ten minutes she would pour herself a cup of coffee, but for now all she wanted was to relax. For this reason and that she hadn't had a break since she'd started. It was now three o'clock, and all she wanted was peace and calm and quiet. This was bliss! The knots in her nerves were starting to untie.

She heard the door open.

No way was she going to get up. She opened one eye and there was Gray. Her first reaction was to take her feet off the table—she must look awfully inelegant. But she didn't move them. Her feet needed a rest.

'If the building's on fire, then I'll move,' she mumbled. 'But otherwise I'm staying here till my feet tell me I can move.'

'That doesn't sound like the voice of a star of the silver screen,' he said. 'But stay there anyway. Don't be alarmed.'

Her eyes were still closed, and why should she be alarmed? She heard the scrape of a chair on the other side of the coffee-table, and then her right foot was grasped firmly, lifted and moved. Two thumbs pressed into her sole.

Her eyes flashed open. 'What are you doing? I...oooh!'

He was sitting in a chair opposite her, bent over her foot which was now in his lap. And he was hurting it! No, he wasn't—after the initial shock she decided that what he was doing was very, very nice indeed. He was bending, pressing, massaging. 'That's wonderful,' she said, and it was.

'Lie back and relax. I'll get the muscles eased a bit, get the blood flowing. You've been on your feet for too long.'

He started to squeeze the other foot. Once again there was that first impression of pain, followed by contentment. Eyes still shut, she said lazily, 'You're supposed to be an oncologist, not an expert on massage. Where did you learn to do this?'

'I used to be a runner—a hurdler, in fact. It's a sport in which your feet take quite a battering. The physiotherapist used to do this for me—and it felt so good that I got her to teach me how.'

'I want you to teach me.' Something suddenly struck her. 'What did you say just now—about the silver screen?'

'Ah. That's why I came to see you. Some kind soul at the Residency fetched me out of my room, and said that yesterday's charity performance was coming on TV. So I watched, and saw you knocking me into that disgusting green stuff. Did you know the cameras were there?'

His tone was carefully neutral, so she couldn't tell if he was pleased or not. 'Too right I knew,' she said. 'The more exposure we get on TV, the more money the charity will get. I don't mind making a fool of myself for a good cause. Do you?'

'Falling in the gunge wasn't all. Everyone saw me kissing you.'

'Well, it wasn't so bad, was it? A bit green-gungy, but otherwise quite a nice kiss, I thought. Put it this way, I'm not going to accuse you of sexual harassment.'

'You're too good to me,' he muttered. Gently, he laid her feet back on the table. 'Stay there a bit longer,' he said, 'and I'll fetch you a coffee.'

'I'll let you,' she told him. 'My feet are very grateful, but they're insisting on their full fifteen minutes' break.' She thought a minute. 'Did you come over here just to say we'd been on TV together? That was good of you.'

'I don't understand your English programming yet, but apparently the programme will be repeated this evening. I thought you might like to watch yourself.'

'I'll phone my father, he can record it for me.'

She kept her feet on the table, but she opened her eyes now. He handed her a cup of coffee, then sat opposite her again. He didn't say anything at first. She had noticed this earlier—sometimes he would wait for quite some time before speaking. She wondered if it was an Australian custom.

Eventually he said, 'Earlier you mentioned that you had been a cook. And I can see that you're a bit older than I'd expect an SHO to be. There must have been some kind of gap between leaving school and starting medicine. D'you want to tell me why?'

Did she want to tell him? She thought she did; she didn't mind this man knowing about her. 'When I left school I wasn't sure what I wanted to do. So I wandered round the world for five years—I told people I was spending my young-age pension. Then I decided that I wanted to study medicine and came back to England.'

'A bit irresponsible, wasn't it? The average British male doctor will work for forty years. The average British female doctor works for only thirty-five years. After all your training, will you only work for thirty years?'

'Are you objecting to female doctors?' she asked heatedly. 'Because from what I've seen, they do more when they are at work than male doctors do.'

'Not objecting,' he said calmly, 'just making a valid observation.'

'Seemed a bit prejudiced to me,' she grumbled, 'but I suppose you're entitled to your opinion. To answer your question, I don't think my five years out were irresponsible. The experiences I had made me a better doctor.'

'That could well be.' He stood and stretched. 'I tend to be a bit of a puritan about work. Whatever you do—work or play—if you don't do it with total dedication, total commitment, then it's not worth doing at all. I don't too much mind a young doctor who doesn't know something, he—or she—can learn in time. But I can't stand a doctor who is slapdash, or casual.'

She thought about this for a moment. 'Is that a warning?' she asked.

'Certainly not. It's a simple statement.' He stood. 'See you tomorrow morning, Lucy. I see we're on duty together.'

After he had left she slipped her shoes back on, then stood and stretched. Another couple of hours and she should be off. It had been a tiring day. What Gray had said intrigued her, though she wasn't quite sure why he had said it. But she did not have time to think about it yet. She had work to do.

Like Gray, Lucy too lived on site, in one of the small staff flatlets. Her basic training had been in a south London hospital, and she had rented a flat near there but it was too far to commute to Lizzie's. Her father had a large house quite close to Lizzie's—in fact she had a bedroom and kept quite a few clothes there. She could have lived with him, but years of self-sufficiency had made her want a place of her own.

In fact she liked her little bedsitting room, with its tiny adjacent shower room. It was just sufficiently luxurious to make her feel pampered. She had added the few little personal possessions that made it seem a home and not just a room. There were books, cushions, dried flowers, and one wall was covered with a vast collage of photographs taken in her wanderings. She was happy here. But she knew one day she'd leave easily and without any regrets.

She showered, dressed casually in a tracksuit and lay on her bed to read. The past two days had been strenuous—in an hour she'd make herself a light supper and then go early to bed.

Her mobile phone rang. She looked at it with distaste, but, as only a handful of people knew her number, she picked it up anyway. It would be someone she wanted to hear from.

'Hi, James here,' a voice said. 'I need you urgently tonight. Say in half an hour?' Her brother James. Not a man to waste words.

She checked her watch—well, it was only seven o'clock. Still… 'But I'm exhausted,' she said. 'I was looking forward to an early night.'

'Doctors aren't entitled to be exhausted. You got me into this job, I'm doing it and I need you tonight. It's the charity "do" at the Cleveland Rooms. I told you they needed a handful of personable young women like you for the main event.'

She didn't know whether to sigh or smile at James' words. He was making fun of her, she knew. But they were good friends.

'I thought that Marion was going to be the personable young woman that you supplied,' she said, referring to James' wife, 'and when I talked to her she seemed very keen.'

'She was, she is very keen. But she's got to take things very easy for a week or two. Doctor's orders. She's in bed.'

She guessed what he meant at once. 'Doctor's orders! James, am I going to be an auntie? How many months is she gone? You should have told me!'

James' manner of speaking was always dry, but she was his sister, she knew him. He was delighted. 'Making you an auntie, though very important, was not the most important consideration. But she's now three months gone, and she'd be very pleased if you came round for a medical and female conversation.'

'I'll phone her tomorrow.'

'Good. I take it you'll change at Dad's; I'm sending Francis Ponder round to pick you up.'

'I don't want to be picked up by Francis! He drinks too much.'

'I know he does. But if you catch him when he's sober he's quite interesting. And he's rich, he has contacts, he's useful and he's keen on you. And I'm certain you can handle him.'

'All right. I'll be waiting outside in thirty minutes.'

She rang off. This was not going to be the quiet evening she had been looking forward to.

Her older brother James was an economist. He lectured at Cambridge, he advised the Government, he was the author of reports on Third World debt. A couple of years ago he had told her that someone high in the health service had asked him to help out with the organisation of a hospital charity, and he'd intended to refuse. She had persuaded him that it was a worthy cause, and whatever she could do to help, she would. So he had taken the position, and the charity, like every organisation that James touched, had profited enormously.

She pulled an anorak over the tracksuit, grabbed a bag and went downstairs. She would wait for Francis in the open air. He wasn't the companion she would have picked—but James had shown her that there were times when personal considerations didn't matter.

'Wearing a tracksuit? You're not going out exercising again?'

Somehow he'd walked up behind her. She had been admiring the evening London sky, trying to name the buildings whose spires, towers, roofs she could see. And Gray Woods had caught her, gazing open-mouthed.

'No...no,' she said, slightly uncomfortable and not sure why. 'I'm just going out with a friend for a couple of hours...where have you been?'

'Over onto the ward. Young Mary Peterson is... Forget work for now, Lucy. It'll still be there when you go in tomorrow.'

'I like Mary, and her parents are decent people. Mary's getting worse, isn't she?'

'She could be better, and that's the last word I'm going to say.' He smiled at her. 'You're tougher than I thought. You had a hard day yesterday, you've worked all day on the ward today and still you're going out. I've taken things easy most of today and I'm still shattered.'

'Yes, well, I…'

Francis could have timed things better. Why didn't he arrive after Gray had gone inside? And did he have to make such a show? Perhaps he did; Francis was Francis.

A plum-coloured Rolls-Royce murmured to a stop beside them. Out of it stepped Francis, in a white silk dinner jacket, a gardenia in his lapel.

'Lucy, my love!' Francis tried to hug Lucy, to kiss her. She submitted to the hug, turned her cheek for the kiss.

'Francis, behave yourself! I work here.'

'Of course you do, dear, and what a place it is. Come, let me whisk you away and you can change out of that dreadful maroon thing you're wearing.'

She looked at him suspiciously. 'You haven't been drinking, Francis?'

'I haven't touched a drop. Not yet, but I intend to make up for it. Come, come, come!'

She wondered whether to introduce the two men standing by her. Perhaps not—they didn't seem to have much in common. Glancing at Gray, she decided it would be a very bad idea. His face was like stone. Francis obviously hadn't made a very favourable impression on him. Francis, of course, hadn't even noticed Gray's existence.

'Bye, Gray,' she said, stepping into the Rolls. 'See you in the morning.'

He didn't reply. And as the car slid forward she turned to see him motionless, staring after them.

Her father's house was quite close. Francis steered expertly into the cobbled back yard; parking at the front was quite impossible. Lucy quickly kissed her brother and father, deposited Francis with them and ran upstairs. She had friends who would take the entire afternoon to prepare for a function like this; she gave herself fifteen minutes.

In her bedroom were what she called her working clothes. The things she wore when she was out at some boring formal function. She'd already decided on the white cocktail dress she was going to wear, and it was the work of a minute to slip it on, to brush her hair and apply slightly more make-up than she normally liked. Pendant earrings, a string of pearls that had been her mother's and she was ready.

Her father wasn't coming—he said he was too old and besides he had someone from the House coming to see him. Francis drove her and her brother to the Cleveland Rooms, and she decided that, even though at the moment his driving was expert, Francis was not going to drive them back. They drove down Park Lane, heading for the King's Road.

'What's the function this time, Francis?' she asked. She had to admit, Francis excelled at persuading people in the public eye to offer their services for free.

'Of all things, it's a fashion parade,' Francis said excitedly. 'All the big glossy magazines are sending photographers, all the national dailies, too. Ebeneezer Gil, you know that exciting designer everybody's raving about, he's letting us try on some of his new collection. Lots of tickets sold, lots of Press, lots of publicity, lots of excitement.'

'Lots of money for hospital charities,' her brother said quietly.

'Exciting new designer Ebeneezer Gil,' Lucy muttered to herself. 'I've seen his dresses before, they're more hole than cloth. I'm glad I'm wearing my sturdy knickers.' This was not going to be her idea of a good time.

First there was a reception. She told Francis that she wanted an orange and soda with ice, and, no, she did not want a vodka dropping in it. Then she wandered round, saying hello to the people she knew. It was important to keep an eye open for photographers; if they were nearby she smiled automatically. A gloomy face would stand out. She was introduced to new people, shook hands, said how happy she was to support this very deserving charity. And all the time she was conscious of James and Francis, working the room in their own way.

After a while she was shepherded into a changing room, and a couple of dressers helped her into a silver creation that she wouldn't have accepted as a gift. Fortunately there weren't any holes. Unfortunately, there wasn't any waist.

'Nice to dress a girl from one of the larger sizes, isn't it?' sniffed one dresser, ignoring Lucy completely.

'Someone with a bit of body on her,' agreed the other. Lucy decided to take this as a compliment.

She had never lacked confidence, and so happily paraded down the makeshift catwalk, pirouetted and smiled. Flashbulbs exploded around her. Later on, still in the same outfit, she had to pose with a group of other amateur models, and then sit on someone's knee. By now she knew her smile was getting a bit forced.

Finally, there was more to drink, a plate of the inevitable canapés and one or two speeches. The speeches were fortunately short. Then she could fairly go home, her work was done. She went back to the changing room and struggled back into her own dress, for the dressers were now more interested in packing what she had taken off than helping her.

'I think we've done rather well,' James said as she talked to him in a little back office. 'More than a few large cheques, and, most important, the promise of some long-term sponsorship. I'm very pleased. Thanks for what you did, Lucy. And I gather you were taking part yesterday as well.'

'My pleasure,' she said. 'I enjoyed yesterday more than tonight.'

'Tonight will earn more money. Fund-raising is an industry, little sister. You have to do what is necessary.'

'I know, I just don't like it.'

'Who's off for another drink, then? What a very successful evening, I enjoyed every minute!' Francis burst into the room.

'I've got a couple of hours' work here still,' James said. 'But if you could see to Lucy…'

'I want to go straight back to the hospital,' Lucy said. 'I've got work in the morning. And, Francis, I've watched you drinking, you are not to drive anywhere.'

'Perhaps not. Then shall we share a taxi?'

'I'll see you in the foyer in exactly five minutes,' Lucy said. 'I just want a quick word with James.'

'At your command. I'll go and snare a taxi.'

'Quick,' Lucy said, 'I haven't had time for a private word all night. How's Marion and why is she in bed?'

'The doctor said no need to worry,' James said, smiling hugely. 'She picked up a bug somewhere, had a touch of food poisoning—I think she'll be able to get up tomorrow.'

'No need to worry, then.' Lucy was happy for James and Marion and she knew her father would be delighted. He wanted grandchildren.

Marion was a year younger than her. With a frown Lucy began to think of the girls she had been at school with—how many of them did she know now with families of their own? Practically all of them. Hmm. Still, she had her career. She dismissed the thought.

They set off in the taxi. As usual, Francis had had too much to drink, perhaps far too much to drink. 'Stay in your own half of the seat,' she warned him as he lurched towards her. 'I'm tired and I'm not in the mood.'

Francis got the message, at least until the taxi pulled up outside her little block of flats. 'Wait for me,' he said, thrusting notes at the taxi driver, and carefully climbed out.

'Francis,' she said warningly, but Francis was not going to be denied—he put his arms round her and tried to kiss her.

More irritated than anything, she put her hands on his chest and pushed him off. She must have been more tired than she thought. As she pushed her heel caught on the kerb edge, and she tripped and fell backwards. The side of her dress caught on the edge of a wooden seat, and ripped. The breath rushed out of her as she landed heavily on the pavement.

She wasn't really hurt, but she was blazingly angry. And then things got even worse. Another coincidence—yet again Gray Woods walked over from the direction of the hospital.

He looked at Francis, and at her on the ground. 'Are you all right, Dr Brett?' he asked icily.

'Fine, thank you,' she said, trying to see just how badly her dress was torn. 'I often lie on the pavement when I'm coming home.'

Too late she realised it was the wrong thing to say. 'I'm sure you do,' he said. 'May I help you up?'

He extended his hand, but she ignored it and scrambled to her feet.

'Look, my antipodean friend,' said Francis, 'we can do without your help. Now why don't you shove off?' Then he made what Lucy knew was a big mistake. He tried to push Gray bodily away.

She winced at what happened next. Gray punched Francis, apparently not very hard, in the stomach. Francis said, 'Oof,' and sat down on the pavement. Lucy sighed. This evening had started badly, now it looked like turning into a nightmare.

She dragged Francis to his feet, propelled him towards the waiting taxi. 'You deserved that,' she stormed at him. 'Now go home and sober up.' When Francis looked like objecting, she snapped, 'I said go!' The taxi pulled away.

She turned to Gray. 'There was no need to hit him,' she said. 'I could have handled him perfectly well.'

'It looked like it. That man was drunk and didn't know what he was doing. Who was he, anyway? Your boyfriend—some young man with more money than sense? You pick your men with care, don't you?'

There were just too many accusations, too many things he had wrong. 'I've dealt with drunks before,' she said, her voice shaking with anger. 'As a medical person I try to do it with my voice, not my fists. You should try it sometimes.'

'He had already pushed you to the floor, and was trying to do the same to me. He needed a shock, so I gave him one.' He looked at her carefully. 'You're holding your side. Are you in pain at all? Would you like me to look at…?'

'No, I am not in pain, and all I want to look at is your disappearing back. Goodnight, Dr Woods.'

She walked to the front door, and he remained standing. As she fumbled for her key she thought of something. She turned and walked back to him. 'You'd just been over to the main building—why?'

'I was called out again to see Mary Peterson.'

She didn't want to know any more. She went up to her room, glad that he didn't follow immediately behind.

CHAPTER THREE

WHEN Lucy arrived on the ward next morning she found Gray already there in Sister's office. Today he had on dark trousers, a rose-coloured shirt and a tie with teddy bears. He looked cool, efficient, completely relaxed. The very sight of him made her feel uncomfortable. Unusually for her, she hadn't slept well.

He didn't smile or say good morning. 'I was just talking to Lisa about Mary Peterson,' he said. 'I'm afraid things aren't looking well. I'd like you to phone her parents and make sure they're coming on this morning. I'd like to see both if possible.'

'I'll see to it,' she said, her tongue feeling thick.

'There's something in my locker I want you both to see,' Lisa said happily, apparently oblivious of the atmosphere. 'I'll just fetch it.'

They were left alone, which Lucy didn't particularly want. She couldn't help herself; she yawned, hugely.

'It's nice to have your body here,' he said coolly. 'I trust your mind is here, too. Are you sure you can keep awake?'

He was entitled to that; she deserved what he said. 'I'll be fine,' she muttered. Then she leaned to pick a file from Lisa's desk, and dropped it. Papers fluttered downwards and she scrabbled to gather them together. He merely looked at her.

Lisa bounced back in. 'There's a lovely picture of

you in the paper, Lucy. I don't think Gray has seen it.' She opened the paper and spread it on her desk. Lucy looked down and nearly groaned. It was a good picture. There she was in a happy embrace with Francis, smiling, bright-eyed, a champagne glass in her outstretched hand. She looked the picture of a party girl. There was no way of telling that there was only orange juice in the glass.

'She looks very fetching,' Gray said. 'It's good to see staff having a good time. Now, if we can get on?'

At long last Lisa realised there was an atmosphere. 'I've got things to do on the ward,' she said, and left.

Gray pushed the newspaper across to Lucy. 'You might like to keep this,' he said. 'Precious memories and so on.'

Lucy gave an elaborate shrug. 'Not really. I've got so many others.'

'I'm certain you have.' He looked at the newspaper again, and then said, his voice rising in disbelief, 'What's this? It says here you're Lady Lucy Brett. A Lady?'

What else could go wrong? Why did he have to find out now? She had met too many men who had a problem with her title. 'I *am* a Lady.'

'Remarkable! And a doctor as well? Now, I'm not sure how things run in England, but in Australia we expect dedication to the job. SHOs get little enough sleep anyway, they can't afford to waste time drinking the night before they're expected to do a full day's work. Even if they are Ladies.'

She asked, 'Don't you think it would be better to wait until I've done something wrong before reminding me of the necessity for dedication?'

'No, I don't. You're not fully competent this morning, and I see no reason to wait till you've made a mistake to point this out. Now. Can we get on with my round?'

Adam Harrison, the consultant, was away that week, so Gray led the ward round on his own. Each patient was visited, and it was Lucy's job to present the case and have ready all the relevant files and paperwork. Fortunately she didn't make any large mistakes. She noticed that, even though Gray might be angry with her, he was kindness itself to all their charges. At end of round, he nodded to her curtly. 'Everything appears to be in order.'

'I'll try to keep it that way,' she said bravely, and set off for the doctors' room to start on the paperwork.

Three hours later she was back on the ward and she desperately needed a coffee. But as she walked on to the wards she saw John Ryan, sitting on his bed again. The other three boys, she knew, were having lessons. And from the hunched way John was sitting, he wasn't very happy.

'John? Have you got a minute? There's a couple of things I want to ask you.'

He looked up, concealing his pleasure with his habitual apparent indifference. 'I'm not doing anything much right now,' he said. 'What is it?'

She walked over and sat by his bed. 'You know I told you I used to be a cook?' she said. 'Well, I've brought you a few photographs and details. See if it's the kind of thing you're interested in. I thought you might like to think about applying for a course, for when you get out of here.'

'When I get out of here? When's that likely to be?'

'It might be sooner than you think. But whenever

it is, you've got to start thinking about the future. Now, I'd no idea about cooking, but this is where I got my first job...'

Talking about food wasn't a good idea—all it did was remind her of her own rumbling stomach. But after a slow start she saw that John was getting really interested. He asked good questions, genuinely wanting to know more about her career. She just didn't have the heart to leave him.

After a while his mates came back from their lesson. She looked at her watch, dismayed; time had passed too quickly. Not even chance of a standing drink. Perhaps she could beg some chocolate off Lisa. But now there were the bloods to do.

In the middle of the afternoon, as she took the last specimen of blood, she turned to see Gray looking at her. His expression was odd.

'Time for a coffee break,' he said. 'Whatever you're doing can wait for fifteen minutes.'

'Are you sure drinking coffee doesn't mean I'll be falling down on the job?' she asked sweetly. 'After all, I've got to live up to your exacting Australian standards.'

He came over, took the little bottle from her hand, and, before she realised what he was doing, had lifted her bodily and turned her round. She didn't know he was so strong! And where his hands had grasped her, under the arms, she felt...strange.

'Coffee,' he said. 'I want to clear the air a bit. We've got to work together, so let's see how we can arrange it. And perhaps I've been...' He stopped, as if thinking.

'A positive pain in the backside?' she suggested,

and took some pleasure when he closed his eyes in exasperation.

They reached the doctors' room, and she accepted the coffee he gave her with tremendous gratitude. It was life-restoring. He sat opposite her and said bluntly, 'You didn't have any lunch.'

'I often don't have any lunch.'

'I had to come back onto the ward. I saw you talking to young John Ryan, I even heard a bit of what you were telling him. You gave up your lunch-time, not for any medical reason, but to make him feel happy.'

'People are people, not cases,' she said. 'You have to talk to them.'

'Possibly. But...'

A junior nurse tapped on the door, and poked her head round it. 'Could I get Maddy Brown's case notes for Sister, please?' she asked, and came in when Gray waved at her to enter.

'This is like back home,' he said when the nurse had gone. 'We're never going to get chance to have a long conversation without being interrupted.'

Greatly daring, Lucy said, 'If we're going to make it up like chums in Mallory Towers School, and you want to talk uninterrupted, then why don't we have a drink tonight?'

After a pause, 'Yes,' he said, 'I think that's a good idea.'

She knew he did not know his way around yet. 'There's quite a pleasant pub about half a mile up the road, just behind the white stone church. Called The Pheasant. How about meeting there about nine?'

'Sounds fine. Are you a red wine or a white wine person?'

'Red,' she said, 'and I like it oaky.'

'There's a very good Coonawarra Valley,' he said, 'if they have it.' He paused. Then, 'I've never had a drink with a real live Lady before.'

'Oh, I've drunk with Australians,' she told him. 'I've got a bush hat with corks dangling from it and you can call me Sheila.'

'Don't push it,' he said.

She felt a bit apprehensive, a bit excited that night. She wasn't quite sure what to wear, and decided on a dress for a change, a pleasant blue floral one. She took a little more care than usual with her make-up, and slipped on white leather heels.

He was already waiting when she walked into The Pheasant, in a little booth at the far end. He stood as she approached him. She saw that he had made an effort too; he was wearing light trousers, and a dark woollen jacket, with a fashionable darker grey shirt. She felt pleased that he wanted to dress well for her. Or perhaps he always dressed this way at night. It struck her that she knew so little about him.

They sat at each side of the booth, he indicated an open bottle in front of them, and two glasses. 'Not the Australian wine I wanted, but a Rioja. I think you'll like it.'

He poured them each a glass, and she sipped. Just how she did like it, rich and full of body. 'This is good,' she said. 'First drink I've had for a week.'

He looked at her, puzzled. 'But you were out last night. I saw the picture of you, with the glass in your hand.'

'Orange juice or tonic water. When I'm working, I never drink anything else.'

'Working? You were at a party.'

'It's still work,' she told him. 'You're on display, you have to put forward the right attitude, show the right smile. And, believe it or not, a jamboree like last night is not my idea of a good time. I'd rather be in a place like this, with a couple of friends.'

'Yes,' he said thoughtfully. 'As a matter of fact, I've got a confession to make. I had lunch with Melissa Yates, the neurology registrar, and I showed her the photograph of you. She told me a couple of things I didn't know. Apparently this charity you work for makes a tremendous amount of money. It does an awful lot of good.'

'We aim to,' she said gently. 'Don't forget you did your bit on Saturday.'

'Perhaps so. But you don't know the worst of it. My stay here in England is sponsored by that very same charity. Last night you were out working for me.'

'I was happy to,' she assured him. 'But please don't thank me, I'm feeling a bit fragile and I might burst into tears.'

'I always pay my debts eventually. And I think I'm in your debt.'

Something struck her, something he had said. 'You said you showed my picture to Melissa,' she said. 'Where did you get it from?'

'The shop in the hospital entryway,' he told her blandly. 'I bought a paper specially.'

They drank their wine in silence for a couple of minutes.

'Tell me about being Lady Lucy Brett,' he said. 'Does it make you feel—well, different?'

She laughed. 'Not very. My great-great-something

grandmother slept with Charles the Second. He was very grateful, so he made my great-great-something grandfather a marquis. The title wasn't won on a battlefield, but in a bed. Other people are impressed by it, though. So I use it. Now tell me about your ancestry.'

'Ah,' he said. 'I'm descended from one of the original Australian settlers. In fact he was a convict, transported for sheep stealing.'

'Can't have been very bright, can he?' she asked. 'Imagine being caught stealing a sheep.'

He looked at her in astonishment a minute, then laughed. 'Lucy, you have a way with words.'

She was enjoying herself, much more than she had expected to. She wanted to know more about him. Perhaps he would tell her more.

But he was curious about her too. 'I want to ask you a personal question,' he said. 'Do you mind?'

'It depends. Probably not, what is it?'

'Is your family rich?'

'Yes,' she said simply. 'Well, my father is and both my brothers do very well.'

'So why did you become a doctor? Did you not think that someone else could have used your training? I know you're a good SHO, but...'

'But you think I should have given up my place in medical school to someone who was not studying it as a hobby?' Now she was really angry. 'Dr Woods, your judgemental arrogance is matched solely by your stupidity. I trained to be a doctor because it's something I wanted to do, and something I thought I'd be good at. You can condemn me when I've done something wrong, but not before. Now, if you'll excuse me, I've got work to do.' She stood and marched out.

Unfortunately, the pub door wasn't one she could slam.

'We thought she just had a sore throat, Doctor,' Mrs Allen said tearfully. 'I gave her some lozenges to suck, and then when it didn't get better I took her to our GP. He said it was probably pharyngitis and we weren't to smoke near her or give her spicy food. But it didn't get better and somehow…somehow we had to come here. Has she got cancer?'

Lucy looked down at six-year-old Mary Allen, obviously terrified and clutching her mother's hand. This was always difficult, for she didn't want to terrify the distraught Mrs Allen, but neither did she want to give her false hope.

She glanced at the results of the blood count she had ordered. Low haemoglobin and platelet count, but a very high white count. The conclusion was almost inevitable. Mary had acute leukaemia.

Choosing her words with care, she said, 'Mary's blood needs attention—she's anaemic. We'll treat the throat with intravenous antobiotics, and see to the blood as well. Then we'll have a bone marrow aspirate—that means we take a tiny sample from one of her bones, and it tells us exactly what is wrong. Then she'll probably need chemotherapy.'

'Bone marrow? She's got leukaemia, hasn't she?' Mrs Allen's voice was near breaking.

Lucy hated this part of the job. But it was necessary. 'Mrs Allen, your daughter is ill. But we can treat her.' Lucy had been told never to use the word cure, unless she was absolutely certain she meant it. 'Now, what your daughter needs is comfort and reassurance from you. You've got to be strong for her. If she sees you are upset—then she will be upset. So smile at her!'

Somehow, Mrs Allen did as she was told. Lucy could see the signs of the internal struggle, and guessed what the woman was going through. 'I'll be all right,' Mrs Allen said. She bent over, kissed her daughter. 'We'll be all right, won't we, darling?'

Mary said nothing.

'Sit here for a while,' Lucy said. 'I'll have a coffee brought out to you, and later we can talk again.' She hesitated, looked from patient to mother. Mrs Allen wiped her tears with a handkerchief, straightened her shoulders. She'd cope, Lucy decided.

It was always a terrible shock when parents realised their child had cancer. There was something final about the word itself. The fact that so many childhood cancers were now completely curable didn't seem to bring much solace.

But most parents did cope. One of the smaller pleasures of working on this ward was to see the toughness with which so many families dealt with the serious illness of a child.

She walked into the corridor and Lisa beckoned her. 'A visitor for you,' she whispered. 'I've put him in the doctors' room.' For a second she wondered if Gray had come across specially to see her but that would be silly, he wasn't a visitor. She opened the door, and there was Francis. He was holding a vast bunch of flowers. 'What are you doing here?' she asked coldly. 'Can't you see I'm busy?'

'You haven't answered my calls to your mobile,' he told her. 'I wanted to apologise, so I've brought you a bunch of flowers and I'm sorry for acting like an idiot.'

She had to admit, it was handsomely said. 'It doesn't matter, you're forgiven,' she said. 'Now...'

The door opened and in came Gray. She saw his eyes flick from her to Francis to the flowers. What more can happen to ruin my day? she wondered.

'I believe you have duties on the ward, Dr Brett,' Gray said icily. 'If you could manage to keep your social life separate from your professional life, then I feel sure that everyone would benefit.'

'Off you go, Lucy,' Francis said. 'Dr Woods and I have a little unfinished business.'

'Francis!'

'As your friend said, off you go, Dr Brett.'

She had to leave them. If they were going to play Man games, then let them.

She looked after, cared for, all her charges. But inevitably there were some who came to mean more to her than most. Mary Peterson had been such a one. Usually her condition was curable but for some reason Mary just didn't respond. For long enough now, everyone had known what would shortly happen. Mary's parents were by her bedside, so was the hospital clergyman. And it was he who slipped through the curtains round the bed and quietly asked Lucy if she would come. Mary was dead.

There were procedures to follow, paperwork to be completed. The nursing staff would see to Mary, and the clergyman took her parents away. After an hour it seemed as if Mary had never been there.

Lucy's duties on the ward could wait a while; she

was entitled to some time to herself. She went to the doctors' room, and there lying on the table was Francis' bunch of roses. Francis, of course, had long since gone. The flowers looked as if they had been placed in remembrance of someone. She sat on the couch and wept.

Gray came in. He seemed to have an instinct for turning up just at the wrong time. She lifted her tear-streaked face and looked at him. 'Mary Peterson?' he asked.

She nodded. 'I know it happens, I know we shouldn't get too involved, I know we can't feel for everybody. But at times I'm entitled to a bit of self-indulgence. And it's not fair!'

'We have to get involved,' he told her. 'We'd be poor doctors otherwise. And what you're feeling isn't self-indulgence.'

He came to sit by her, and put his arm round her shoulders. It wasn't what she expected, she didn't even know if it was what she wanted, but it was comforting. His body was warm, there was the musky smell of a cologne, but underlying it the scent of maleness. She leaned her head into him, and wrapped her arm round his waist. He stroked her hair.

After a while she felt better, embarrassed even. He said nothing as she took her head away, but offered her a white linen handkerchief. She wiped her eyes, then looked in dismay at the mascara marks. 'I'll wash it,' she said.

'Whatever. Like a coffee?'

'Yes, please. We seem to live on coffee.'

'All hospital doctors do.' It was a banal conversation, but it helped her.

He brought her coffee, and they sat side by side again. 'How did you get on with Francis?' she asked.

'We got on very well—in fact, we shook hands. He wanted to apologise as much to me as to you. I quite like him, he's a very astute man when he's sober. I gather he's known you for quite some time. Why does he drink so much?'

'I don't know, he's apparently happy and successful. Male behaviour never fails to amaze me.'

'You amaze me, Lucy. Everything you've done since you pushed me into that tank has amazed me.' He put his coffee-cup back on the table, and the tinging noise it made echoed—and echoed—and echoed.

For a moment longer they sat side by side, hips and shoulders touching. He was looking at her, and she noticed his eyes were grey—like his name, she thought inconsequentially. His eyes were intent; they seemed to darken as he stared at her. She knew what he was going to do, and she wanted him to do it.

He had kissed her before, but that had been in the heat of the moment, when he had been excited, perhaps even angry. Now he kissed her gently, their lips barely touching. It was so good!

Her eyes drooped and closed, her limbs felt powerless. She sank deeper into the cushions of the couch. His arm came across her body, caressed her shoulder. Then he was leaning over her, pulling her body closer. She felt the soft pressure of his tongue and opened to him; she reached for him and felt the tension of him. Suddenly, theirs was the kiss of two lovers, demanding and giving at the same time. Her safe, ordered world had gone; she only knew her need for the man holding her.

His hand slipped onto her breast, and she gasped with urgency. She wanted him to…and then slowly, reluctantly, he released her. 'I didn't mean that to happen,' he said.

She tried to be flippant. 'Are you sorry, then? There's no real need to be.' She was trying to make little of what had just occurred. But she knew that they had ventured onto something new—something new, frightening and perhaps dangerous.

She thought he felt the same way. He looked perplexed, as if something had happened out of his control. 'What are we going to—?' he started, but she interrupted him. Just now, she didn't want to think, to make plans.

'We both got carried away a bit, so forget it,' she said. But she knew she couldn't forget it, and she doubted that he could.

'You know that neither of us can do that.' She should have guessed that he would never back away from a confrontation.

'No. But we have to work together and—'

Never had she been so pleased to be interrupted. The usual knock on the door, and then Lisa appeared. 'Dr Woods, Martin Track's parents are here. They say you wanted to see them.'

Lucy stood, hoping that her face or hair didn't betray in some way what had just happened. 'They can come in here, Lisa. I've finished my coffee anyway. See you later, Gray.' And she was gone, striding past Lisa on her way to the ladies' cloakroom. She knew there were repairs she'd have to make.

In fact there weren't. She gazed at her serene face in the mirror. How could she look so unaffected when her mind was in turmoil? Why in turmoil? She'd been kissed before, but never remembered being so affected. What was happening to the tough, resilient Lucy?

CHAPTER FOUR

LUCY knew Gray would come in to see her that afternoon. He was seeing patients in a day clinic some distance away, but she knew it wouldn't take too long. Gray would come to see her.

In fact, it wasn't Gray who came to see her first, but Kenneth Copley. It had to be Kenneth, not Ken, and Lucy suspected he would have much preferred Dr Copley. But ward custom was strong. Christian names for everyone.

Kenneth was the other specialist registrar on the firm, though he wasn't seen too much at Lizzie's, working much of his time at the outlying hospitals. He was married, an older man, who had just come to the realisation that he would never be made consultant. It had made him cynical.

For twenty-five minutes now he had held the increasingly irritable Lucy a prisoner in the doctors' room, telling her that her work would wait and it was more important to listen to him, to learn how the health service 'really worked'. Apparently it worked to prevent Kenneth getting the job he deserved.

It was both a relief and a further irritation when Gray did come in. A relief because she wanted to see him, an irritation because Kenneth showed no signs of going. In fact he seemed to think that he was needed, to make sure she and Gray knew each other. The nerve!

'We're very lucky to have Lucy on our staff,'

Kenneth told Gray. 'Not only is she a good worker, she is a Lady. I think it adds a bit of class.'

'Kenneth, I don't really think that Gray is interested…'

'Oh, but I am,' Gray said, straight-faced, 'I'm absolutely fascinated.'

He's making fun of me, she thought.

Kenneth, of course, never suspected. 'I know that you don't have aristocrats in Australia,' he said, 'but we have them here, and they do a lot of good charitable work. And Lucy's brother does a lot of work for charities too. Any chance of you bringing him in some time, Lucy? I'd like to say hello.'

'He's kept very busy,' Lucy mumbled. She felt herself cringing.

'Well, whenever he has time.' Kenneth glanced at his watch. 'Good Lord. You really shouldn't keep me talking so long, I have a clinic five minutes ago. Bye.'

For a moment, she and Gray sat in silence. 'Sorry about that,' she said eventually. 'I know how you feel about me being a Lady and so on, but Kenneth does tend to get carried away.'

'Not at all. He said you were a good worker and I agree with him. Why did he want to meet your brother?'

'My brother is an economist. Very good at money in the abstract. He's a fellow of a Cambridge college, but he does a lot of work advising the Government. He helps organise the charity I work for—he's very good at it.'

'So he's not just another aristocrat who…'

'Dr Woods, I've told you, not one of my family sits at home playing at being rich! They all work, and so do I! In time I'm going to be a consultant and—'

'All right, all right, I'm sorry. I didn't mean it! I'm even sorry for what I said in the pub, when you flounced out.'

'I did not flounce!'

'You did. You flounced like a master—or a mistress.' He frowned. 'In fact, I think I've read something about a James Brett. Something about him organising money for Third World medical training.'

'That'll be James. He would have picked me up on Sunday night, but his wife is pregnant so he sent Francis.'

'He sent Francis? But I thought Francis was your...'

'My what? My boyfriend?' Lucy roared with laughter. 'Goodness, no. I haven't got a boyfriend, and if I did have, it wouldn't be Francis. I'm far too busy working.'

'But Francis told me that he'd known you for years, that you had an...understanding?'

'We do have an understanding. He understands that I'll turn up at parties with him where I need a partner, but otherwise he's just a family friend.'

Gray was thinking. 'I thought Francis was astute,' he said after a while. 'I didn't realise just how clever he was.'

Lucy glanced at her watch. She'd been here far too long, there were no end of jobs she still had to do. 'I've got to go,' she said, 'but there's something I think I ought to do. Would you like to come to dinner at my father's some time and meet my father and brother, a few other people? You've obviously never met any of the idle British aristocracy—I think you ought to have the chance.'

He looked at her suspiciously. 'You're setting me

up,' he said. 'Whenever you're being sweet I know I'm in for a shock.'

'I'm certainly not setting you up,' she said primly. 'We'd love to hear about sheep shearing and boomerangs and Bondi Beach. Black tie, of course.'

'And I was intending to bring my tucker bag, complete with jumbuck. Yes, I would like to come to dinner. I think.'

'I'll have an invitation sent. Now…'

'One more thing. When you walked, strode, flounced or what out of The Pheasant last Monday, there was half a bottle left. I wasn't going to drink it on my own, so I had it re-corked and it's waiting behind the bar. Can we finish it tonight? We can finish our conversation too.'

She hadn't expected this. After a moment, she said, 'That sounds like a good idea. About nine again?'

'About nine. But you know we live in the same block. Why don't I knock on your door at about a quarter to?'

This was something else. There was a free and easy camaraderie about the hospital flatlets—friends and acquaintances, both male and female, were always dropping in for a chat, for advice, to borrow something. But for some reason the idea of Gray in her room made her nervous. It was…intimate.

'That's a good idea,' she said. 'If I'm not in the room I'll be in the kitchen.' But although he said nothing, she knew he had noticed her hesitation. And she thought he guessed the reason for it.

'My dad had it, so I've got it,' fifteen-year-old Sam Westby said. 'And he died of it so I'll probably die of it. What are you going to do about that?'

'We're probably going to cure you,' Lucy said calmly. 'You've only got stage one—that means that the disease is limited to one region, in your case, the supraclavicular. Neck, to you. We'll treat you first of all with radiation, but chemotherapy is an option.'

Sam thought about this. 'But, like I said, my dad had it and he died—just after I was born.'

'I know, I've talked to your mother about it. We've come a long way in the last fourteen years, we cure more people. And he had stage four—the disease had spread right through him, even to his bone marrow. I think we've caught you in time.'

'So I'm not going to die?'

'I'll be very surprised if you do,' Lucy said, 'and very irritated as well.'

'I wouldn't want to irritate you,' Sam said.

It wasn't an unusual reaction from the older children—usually the boys. They were frightened all right, but they felt they had to be macho, and took refuge in presenting a scornful face to the world, taking a delight in being awkward. Lucy remembered what Gray had said to her as they had walked away from the bed of another very truculent youngster.

'Remember, underneath he's terrified. Being rude is the only way he can cope. We can let him have that.'

Sam had Hodgkin's disease. He had suffered bouts of fever, become anaemic, and when his GP had found enlarged nodes in his neck he had guessed at once what the problem was. Hodgkin's disease struck at the lymphatic system, and if not detected in time could spread through the body, invading the spleen and eventually other organs of the body. No one knew what caused it. But it was usually curable if detected in time. Sam should be all right.

'There's a few lads your own age further up the ward,' Lucy said. 'Why don't you go into the day room and watch telly with them? And don't get into trouble!'

'As if I would,' Sam said, reaching for his dressing gown. 'Any girls there, Doctor?'

Lucy decided that Sam would cope.

It was called displacement activity. You didn't want to think about something, so instead you concentrated on another subject, and pretended it was more important. When Lucy had finished on the ward, she bought a couple of sandwiches from the shop downstairs, intending to eat them in her room. She decided she didn't have time to make her own tea. She didn't completely understand why half the oncologists she knew suggested radiation alone for Hodgkin's disease, and the other half suggested radiation and chemotherapy together. She would read it up in her textbook. So, with sandwich and mug of tea handy, she followed the detailed description of what was known about the causes of the disease.

After three quarters of an hour she realised it wasn't working. She couldn't recall a thing of what she had read. In disgust she slammed the heavy book shut, and went for a shower.

She wasn't going to dress up for him as she had when they'd gone to The Pheasant first. She'd wear the same dark trousers she had worn on the ward all day. But she would change her top. The shirt she had on smelled just a little medical; there was a hint of the ward about it.

Eventually she picked a dark blue silk shirt; it looked well on her. It was a bit revealing, of course, but it showed off her arms, and she was quite proud of her arms. The heavy material clung to her figure— perhaps it was too revealing? She decided to wear it anyhow.

Now there was an hour before Gray would come for her, she knew she could no longer put off thinking about him. This was unlike her. In the past she had always been capable of facing her problems, of reasoning out a solution and then sticking to it. She would do it now. Was Gray a problem?

She had only known him a few days. On the ward she had found him a caring, a competent and a very hard-working doctor. Perhaps too hard-working. She felt he was focused too much, he seemed to think of nothing but his work. She knew he despised doctors—or anyone on the ward—who didn't have his dedication.

Perhaps now he was coming to see that she had a commitment to work equal to his own. But he didn't like her being a 'Lady'. She didn't even know if he liked her. In the past few days he had kissed her twice. The first time had been almost accidental, the second, earlier today, most definitely had not been. Something had flashed between them, some spark, some affinity, some recognition that things between them could go an awful lot further. If the two of them wished. This was the question: did she want a relationship with him?

She knew so little about him. He was here for just six months, then he would go back to Australia. He might even be married! She didn't think so; he didn't act like a married man. But he was very attractive—

perhaps there was a woman already in his life. She decided to ask him when they met later.

As she thought that soon she would see him, that soon he would be in her room, that they would be alone together, she was conscious of a growing excitement. Then the excitement annoyed her. She was nearly thirty, no time to be swooning over a man. But she spent so much time thinking about him!

She had to do something, couldn't just sit and brood. In desperation she went to make herself yet another mug of tea.

She sat at her desk, sipped the tea, forcing herself to be calm. Perhaps now she could make some sense of the causes of Hodgkin's disease. She picked up her book. There was a knock at the door—it couldn't be Gray already! Her heart beat, faster and faster.

It was him. 'I know I'm early. But I found myself sitting in my room, not doing anything, and thinking of nothing but the fact that I was going out with you. So since we're in the same building, I just came.' He looked at the discarded textbook, the mug of tea on her desk. 'You can work too hard, you know.'

'Dr Graham Woods, you are telling me that!' If he only knew how she had passed the last half-hour, how she had been dreaming of him.

'Sorry, it's not like me to object to anyone studying. I'll come back in—'

'Sit down, I'm fed up with work. Could I fetch you a cup of tea?'

He looked at her mug, one she had bought at a hospital fair. There was a painting of a syringe on the side, and the words 'the enema strikes back!' 'I'd like a mug of tea, not a cup,' he said.

She fetched him one. When she returned he was

looking at her collage, at the photographs and post-cards that showed so much of her life over the past fifteen years.

'Europe, Israel, India,' he said. 'South and then North America. But you never visited Australia. I'm surprised at that, it's the home of wanderers.'

'It's on my list,' she said. 'One day I'll go. Perhaps I'll try to work in one of the hospitals there for a year or so.'

'Let me know if you decide. I might be able to help you find a place.'

In six months he would be going back. She didn't want to be reminded of that.

'That's a very fetching shirt,' he said as she handed him the tea. 'But then you always look...' His voice faded away, his expression half assessing, half teasing.

'Go on,' she said. 'I want to be complimented.'

'I was going to say you always look properly dressed for the occasion. But then I realised that the most attractive I've ever seen you look was when you were wet through and had false ears.'

She thought back to her elf outfit, and felt slightly warm. 'I remember that outfit. When it got wet it was almost transparent.'

'Yes. I noticed.'

'A gentleman would have pretended that he didn't notice,' she said sniffily. 'Now, drink your tea, then we'll go down to The Pheasant. Did you want to talk to me about anything in particular?' She felt on edge; she didn't know where this conversation was going.

He, on the other hand, was quite at ease. He sat relaxed on the chair by her desk, his legs crossed in that casual way that only men could get away with.

He had changed into jeans and a tight black sweater, which only served to emphasise the tautness of his muscles, the grace with which he moved. 'We seem to spend half our time sniping at each other on the ward,' he said, 'and I'm anxious to know why. I'm not sure I want to stop it, it makes life interesting. But there's something between us and I'm not sure what. D'you know what I'm talking about?'

Perhaps she should plead ignorance. But she did know what he meant. 'I suppose I do know what you're talking about,' she conceded, 'but are you sure you're not just irritated because you think I'm a social butterfly and yet I'm reasonably competent?'

'That's part of it,' he agreed. 'I've got no family left, my parents died when I was seven and I was brought up in an orphanage. What I am I made myself. It seems strange to have a…ready-made family background. And I suppose a background like yours is bound to irritate me.'

She ignored this last comment. She was looking at him in horror, trying to assimilate the story he had just so casually told her. 'But you told me you were descended from someone transported for sheep stealing. You must have more family somewhere.'

'No. All the other Woods died out. All I've got is a letter written to my grandfather about the transportation. In some ways it's a liberation having no background, Lucy. You make yourself.'

He stood, came over to her and cupped her face in his hands. He kissed her quickly, lightly, on the lips. 'That's three times now,' he said. 'Now, listen, Lady Lucy, you seem to worry about this more than I do. It doesn't matter. And I was brought up by the kindest bunch of people you could wish. I'm on the Board of

Governors of the orphanage now, and I send them a lump of my salary every year.'

'Sometimes I don't know my luck,' she said. 'You had no family. I just upped and left mine for six years.'

'You kept in touch, I don't need them to tell me to know that. Now, how about this red wine?'

'I think I need it,' she said. Conversation with this man tended to veer all over the place. She was learning so much about him. Each little detail, each new facet made him a more enigmatic character. But she'd get to know him in time.

She wrapped a sweater round her neck and they walked downstairs. Instead of their walking down the main road she guided him out of the back of the hospital; there was a short-cut through the back streets that led to the pub. It was dark now, but the streets were well lit.

It happened just as they came to a corner. They both heard the high, panicky woman's voice, 'Get off my bag, it's mine, I...' Then there was a scream, quickly cut off.

They turned the corner. There was a woman on her knees, one hand clutched to her face. The other arm was outstretched, towards a youth who was pulling a handbag off the woman's wrist.

He looked up as the handbag came free and darted off down the empty street at what seemed to Lucy to be an incredible rate. At the far end of the street there were four different darkened openings; once there the youth would be lost. 'Stop thief!' Lucy cried, but there was no one to stop him.

'Look after the woman, Lucy.' Gray's words rapped out, and then he was running down the street.

She thought she had never seen anyone move so fast. On the pavement were three posters in frames. Without losing speed or breaking pace Gray hurdled them, his legs stretching straight and true.

She was a doctor, not a spectator. Lucy hurried to the crouched woman, knelt by her. Reassurance first. She put her arm round the woman's shoulders. 'It's all right, he's gone, you're safe now. I'm a doctor. Don't move yet, just tell me where you hurt.'

The woman lifted a tear-streaked face. 'He hit me,' she gasped. 'I wouldn't let go of my handbag and he hit me.' But Lucy had already seen the graze marks on the woman's cheek.

'Did he only hit you once? Are you hurt anywhere else?'

'My knees hurt where I fell down. And look at my stockings and my skirt! They're ruined.' Painfully the woman stood, looked downwards.

This was a typical reaction, Lucy knew. The woman was shocked, the blood rushing to her core. Shortly she might faint, perhaps even vomit. 'Come and sit on this bench,' she said, urging the woman with an arm round her. 'You'll feel better there, and we'll get you to hospital.'

The woman was now getting hysterical. 'What about my bag? I had the shop takings in it, I was going to the bank.'

Lucy sighed when she heard this. For some time when she was training she had worked in an A and E department, and inevitably come across policemen. They brought in victims, witnesses, asked for cups of tea and hung around hoping for statements. And the stories they told of the foolishness of some people.

Going to the bank with the takings in her handbag, indeed!

'We'll worry about that later,' she said kindly. 'Now...'

'Lucy!' She looked up. Some distance away was Gray, holding, apparently easily, the youth by one hand. 'Use your mobile, ring 999. I'll stay down here.'

She recognised what he was doing, that bringing the youth near the woman would only terrify her. 'Okay,' she shouted back. Trying to keep her body between the woman and the two figures down the street, she opened her own bag. 'What's this street called?' she asked the woman.

After that things moved quickly. First a police car appeared, and one female police officer hurried over to help them as the male officer walked cautiously towards Gray and the youth. Lucy heard the rattle of the officer's radio as she came towards them.

'I'm a doctor,' she said. 'My colleague and I saw this woman being attacked, and her bag was snatched. There was only one thief involved, he's over there.' She nodded to where Gray was talking to the other officer.

'Do we need an ambulance?'

Lucy shook her head. 'I don't think so. This lady should go to hospital for a check-up, but I doubt she's badly hurt. You could take her in your car.' She bent over the woman, who was now looking a little better. 'I'm Dr Lucy Brett. What's your name? Is there anyone you'd like to call?'

'I'm Judy Osmore. If we can call my husband he'll come to pick me up.'

All three looked round as another police car appeared. 'Let's go and sit in the car,' the policewoman said. 'You'll be more comfortable there.'

'I won't have to sit with that man!'

'Of course not,' the policewoman said kindly. 'In fact, he's off to the cells right now.' Lucy looked up to see the youth, now handcuffed, being pushed into the second police car.

'We'll phone your husband and tell him you're being taken to the A and E department at St Michael's,' the policewoman went on. 'We'd like a statement in time but there's no great hurry.'

The policeman joined them, and looked to assess if Judy was capable of answering questions. 'Is this your bag, Ma'am? Could you check it to see if anything has been taken?'

Eagerly Judy seized the bag. 'It's fine! Look, it's still locked.'

'We'd like you to open it and make absolutely sure nothing is missing.'

Judy took a key from her skirt pocket and opened the bag. Inside Lucy could see bundles of bank notes, with bags of silver. 'It all seems to be here,' she said. 'You don't want me to count it now?'

The policeman sighed. 'No, Ma'am. It'll do later.'

The police car holding the thief now drove away, and Gray walked over to them. 'Is the lady all right?' he asked, his eyes flicking over the now slightly more cheerful Judy.

'She's being taken to A and E,' Lucy answered, 'but I don't think there's anything seriously wrong.'

'We can take it from here,' the policeman said. 'I've got your details and there'll have to be statements later. We'll probably call the hospital tomorrow morning.'

'Glad you're all right,' Gray said to Judy. 'The police will look after you now.'

Judy looked up, and Lucy was amused to see that she registered Gray's masculine form, his air of authority. She pushed back her hair, straightened her shoulders, and managed a weak smile. 'Thanks so much for what you did,' she said. 'You're…?'

'I'm Dr Graham Woods. At Lizzie's round the corner. Now, it's time you were in that car and at hospital yourself.'

'We'll be in touch,' the policewoman said. 'You're sure you're both all right?'

'We're fine,' Gray said. 'Though it's been an exciting half-hour.'

He and Lucy watched the police car drive away. 'I think we were going for a drink,' he said.

'We certainly were. But can we go back onto the main road? There's too much excitement down these quiet back streets.'

He took her arm as they walked back to the main road and then along to The Pheasant. She was glad he did. In her time, in the logging camps and in the A and E department, she had seen enough violence. But this had been so unexpected. Her heart was pounding, and she was glad of the warmth and strength of Gray's comforting arm.

He found her a seat in another quiet booth, then went to the bar. Fortunately, there were not too many customers. She did not feel like a noisy, exuberant atmosphere. He returned practically at once, sat opposite her and leaned over to cover her hand with his. She liked it, but she said nothing.

The barman came to the table. On a tray he had

the bottle that they had not finished last time, two wineglasses and two thin glasses filled with a golden liquid. The two thin glasses were set in front of them.

'I think you're a little bit shocked,' Gray said, indicating the glass. 'So I bought us each an Armagnac. Try it, it's good for you.'

She tasted the brandy, and gasped at its strength. But the second sip she enjoyed. She didn't speak till her glass was empty; neither did he. And he was right, she did feel better afterwards.

'Thank you, that was good,' she said. 'It's a pity you can't get it on the National Health.'

'I'm still not accustomed to your health service. But one day I'll try prescribing a bottle of this stuff and see how far we get.'

'You'll not get far,' she told him. 'In fact, you won't get anywhere at all.' She was relaxed now, and she could think over what had happened in the past hour with some degree of calmness. She went on, 'Once I was quite used to this kind of thing. The A and E department I worked in served a city centre area—I saw lots of crime victims. It's just that…on our ward things tend to happen a bit more slowly.'

'I've worked in A and E. I know what you mean.'

Now she was curious about the incident. So much had happened that she hadn't really realised. She wanted to know more. 'Who was the thief? How did you catch him? He might have had a knife or something.' Realisation was striking her. 'You could have been hurt.'

Gray shrugged. 'He was quite fast but there was very little muscle on him. The police knew him at once. I think he's a local drug addict. Anyway, I just caught up with him, stuck my foot out and he tripped over it. He fell and it knocked all the wind out of him. I picked him up and threatened him.'

Her mind went back to what she had seen. 'You saw him and you ran after him. I've never seen anything like it, you were off like a jet while I was still working out what was happening. And you went over those three placards without even breaking pace. You must have been an awfully good runner.'

He pushed the two empty brandy glasses to one side and poured them each a glass of red wine. She thought he was doing this just to avoid having to answer her promptly; in those usually imperturbable eyes she thought she could see sadness. Then, 'I was an awfully good runner,' he said. The flatness of his voice only emphasised the feeling of his words. 'In my event I might have been the best in the world.'

For a while he didn't say anything more, and she didn't want to interrupt his thoughts. He went on, 'I had two ambitions in life, Lucy. I wanted to be a doctor and I wanted to be a champion hurdler. Both need dedication, both need time. But I managed both. I was Australian hurdling champion and I was picked for their Olympic team. Eight weeks before I was due to fly out I fell in training, broke my ankle and, more important, tore all the ligaments. Of course, I missed the Olympics. I was seen by the best orthopaedic consultant in Australia. He told me that, although the ankle would heal, I would never compete in the top rank again. Of course, I tried to prove him wrong. When the bones knitted I trained—how I trained—but my doctor's knowledge told me that he was right. I run for fun every now and again, but that is all.'

She looked at him sadly. 'You spent years of your

life working towards something, and never had the chance even of a trial?'

'It doesn't matter too much, Lucy. The fun is in the trying. There's something about concentrating all your energies on one goal that is rewarding. They were good years.'

After the early excitement she found herself really enjoying the evening. She thought she was getting to know Gray, things about him that had been enigmatic now seemed clear. And the wine tasted good. They sat drinking, opposite each other, in companionable silence.

Then he frowned, even looked slightly wary. He seemed unsure of himself—something she had never expected to see. He'd always been absolutely certain of what he was doing. From a deep pocket on the thigh of his jeans he took an envelope, and placed it on the table between them. He pursed his lips, in doubt.

'I'm intrigued,' she said. 'I don't think I've ever seen you not sure of yourself.'

He laughed. 'The last woman I showed this to thought it was pointless. Perhaps she was right.'

It was the first time he had ever mentioned another woman. For that matter, he'd not told her much at all of his background, and she now knew she wanted to learn more. It might not be the right time, but there were things she had to ask.

'Before we go any further,' she said, 'this might not be the right time, but there are things I've got to ask you. And I can't be bothered to be tactful.'

'Dr Brett can't be bothered to be tactful? Now that is something unusual.'

Lucy felt her face getting rather warm. 'Just because I'm sometimes…direct,' she said, 'doesn't mean that I can't be tactful.' She looked up at his smiling face and decided the only thing to do was rush on. 'Are you married?' she asked. 'And if you're not married, is there some woman waiting for you in Australia?'

She stared down at her drink, not daring to meet his eyes.

'That's a bit forward of you, Dr Brett,' he teased. 'Why do you have to know?'

'You know why I have to know. I could get—interested in you. I'm not saying I *am* interested, just that I could get interested. So tell me.'

Still in his teasing voice, he said, 'I'll tell you one thing. I've never met a woman quite like you before.' Then, in a more serious tone, 'No, there's no one interested in me, no one waiting for me.'

'Why not?' she went on remorselessly. 'You're a good-looking man; you have, as they say, good prospects.'

'There have been a few women in my life. I like women, the company of women. But I've never found one who could understand—could share my dedication. Perhaps I didn't want them to.'

'That's possible,' she agreed. 'Very possible. Sorry to put you through the mincer, but I'm glad we've got things sorted out.'

'So am I. Now it's my turn to work the mincer. Is there a man anywhere waiting for you? If I'm a good-looking man, then you're a very good-looking woman. Why has no one tried to snap you up?'

'I suppose quite a few have. And those that found out that I was a member of the aristocracy were even more keen. But although I've quite liked a few men I've never really fallen for one.'

'Never?'

She thought, and decided to be honest. 'Well, there was a man in America I could have been keen on, but he was older than me, and he was married anyway. We still write to each other occasionally. But I'm still fancy-free. So far I've not found a man I'd like to spend the rest of my life with.'

They looked at each other and laughed. She felt that another barrier between them had been broken down, that they were getting to know each other. He was certainly a good-looking man. Well, perhaps not good-looking so much as...almost without her realising it she found her body reacting to his. She could feel her breasts tighten, a warmth around her neck and temples. She had never felt this way before; her body was betraying her!

She didn't want Gray to know how she felt—well, certainly, not yet. She needed a diversion. Pointing to the envelope on the table, she asked, 'Are you going to show me what is in there?'

'Of course.' Carefully he opened the envelope, took out a transparent plastic sleeve. Inside that she could see a sheet of what looked like cheap writing paper, much handled. 'If you look carefully you can probably read it,' he said. His tone was so neutral that she knew he was hiding something.

She took the plastic sleeve. Yes, she could read the contents. It was a letter, written obviously painfully by someone probably not accustomed to writing. The letters were large and ill formed, there were numerous crossings out. And the message was painfully short.

It was headed Bantock Mining Hospital and dated 19 August 1901.

Dear John,
I am writing to you cos I don't think I will have the chance again. None of our family has ever been much for writing. I was in the mine when there was a rock fall and my leg was broken and is now infected. The doctor is good to me and says I have a chance but we both know I don't have much of one.
I just want to tell you about where you came from, though there isn't much. Your great-great-grandfather, Isaac Woods, was one of the last men to be transported from England, he was condemned in the Oxford Assizes in 1851. He was accused of stealing sheep. That is all I know.
I hope you have a happy life, dear grandson, and that things go well for you.
Your loving grandfather, Cyril.

She looked at him expectantly.
'John Woods was my great-grandfather. This is just about all I have as a family history. My grandfather disappeared very early leaving little more than this letter, and hardly anything is known about my parents either. It was easier to move around in Australia, easier not to leave traces.'
She didn't know what to say. For a while she had thought she was getting to know this man, and now she realised he was as big an enigma as ever. Just what did this letter mean to him? There was only one way to find out. 'What does this letter mean to you?' she asked.

His wineglass was half full; he drained it. 'I used to think it was a kind of talisman. Apart from my stay in the orphanage, this was all the family I had and it was great. I decided other kids were pulled down by relatives, but I was free of them. Then I realised this was a kind of rationalisation. I'd quite like a family— of some sort. Then I wondered if other families would want someone without any relations at all. I'm still not sure about that.'

Choosing her words with care, she said, 'I think most women marry a man, not a family history.'

'But think how important it is when you first meet your future in-laws.'

She had to agree, that was true.

He went on, 'I suppose you know all about your family and your ancestors. Don't you feel different from me?'

'Are you getting at me again?'

'A week ago I would have been. This evening, I am not. I'd like an honest answer, I really would.'

She hesitated, and then said, 'We're all pretty well documented. Nothing gets thrown away—we have household accounts, lists of servants, school reports, doctor's bills, diaries, all sorts of things. I used to think they were a weight, but now I like to know they are there.'

'They make you know who you are?'

She saw the trap he was leading her into. 'I am me, not my family,' she said. 'Just as you are you, with or without a family.'

'But what if I feel different from you? Not better, not worse, but different? What if I think the difference means that we can never really...well, understand each other?'

'Then you're wrong. I'm not like that woman you mentioned who thought this letter is pointless. I can see its point, I can guess what it means to you. But there's far more to you than a...less-than-full family history.'

'Less-than-full family history,' he mocked gently. 'Lucy, you're wasted as a doctor. With your gift for language you should be a writer.'

'With my gift for language I'll tell you what I think of you in a minute,' she threatened. 'Don't make fun of me. Now, the bottle's empty—we're not having another drink, are we? Or do you want another?'

She wanted to get away from the seriousness of the conversation. She had learned an awful lot about him, and she needed time to think about what she had learned.

'We're both working tomorrow,' he said, 'and this evening has been a full one—no, I don't want another drink. Let's walk back.'

This time he didn't take her arm as they walked, he held her hand, and she liked it. She felt they had made progress, that they'd got to know each other a little better.

'Would you like to come to my room for a quick cocoa?' she asked when they reached their little block of flats. 'You could make free of my biscuit barrel as well if you wanted.'

'An invitation few could resist. Yes, I'd love a cocoa. And it'll have to be a quick one.'

Good, he understood the unspoken rules. He was to come for a drink, no more. She sat him on her bed again, and on her player put a CD by an American singer she had come to like—Crystal Gayle. 'Be right back,' she told him, and dashed off to the kitchen.

'You're a romantic,' he told her when she returned with the two steaming mugs. 'And you're not looking forward to a happy love life. I've been listening to the words of her songs—poor old Crystal doesn't seem to be having much luck.'

'Country and western,' she told him, 'always the same themes. Your wife's left you, your dog's died and your truck needs a new engine. When things get tough on the ward I listen to country and western music, and I realise things could be worse.'

'True.' He accepted the mug of cocoa from her, wriggled along the bed so she could slouch by his side. 'But she's got a lovely voice.'

They didn't speak much more then, but sipped the cocoa and ate chocolate biscuits. When he had finished the drink, he stood. 'We're both tired,' he said. 'I'd better go.'

She stood too, and he reached out, pulled her to him. She could feel the length of his body, the leanness, the sense of poised strength being held back. His lips tasted of cocoa—she supposed hers did too. Never mind, it was rather nice. She guessed that he felt the same as she did—this was not the time to push things forward. But now there was definitely something between them. They both knew it. Then for a moment his kiss became more passionate, and she was ready to respond to it. But he eased her away, and sighed. 'I'd better go back to my room.'

CHAPTER FIVE

LUCY found that, if it was managed carefully, most adult patients didn't really mind students coming round to see them. But things were a little different in a paediatric hospital. The oncological consultant, Adam Harrison, realised that students had to learn. But he didn't like the disturbance they could cause on a ward. So he often had a quick ward round, and then called the students together afterwards to talk about what they should have observed.

Lucy always listened too. The students looked ludicrously young to her, but she could learn as well as they could.

'You have just palpated the abdomen of a four-year-old child, Gary Priest,' Adam said. 'What did you find there?'

The student he pointed to licked his lips, and then said, 'A mass in the upper abdomen, irregular in shape. The patient didn't object to being palpated, suggesting that there was no pain or discomfort.'

'Good.' Adam turned to another student. 'Did you notice anything out of the ordinary about the patient?'

'Very white-faced, sir.'

'Which suggests?'

'There are many possible causes, sir. But one is that if the mass is a tumour, there may be bleeding into it. This would produce pallor and hypotension.'

Adam nodded approvingly at the student's caution. 'A good, careful answer. In fact young Gary has a tumour, a neuroblastoma. We have given him an ultrasound and CT scan. Here are the results.' Everyone turned to look at the illuminated pictures on the wall. 'Anyone care to suggest treatment?'

There was silence for a moment, and then the student who had spoken second said hesitantly, 'First a biopsy of the surrounding lymph nodes to see if the tumour has metastasised. If not, then surgical excision.'

'Correct. Both chemotherapy and radiation may be of use if the tumour has spread, but otherwise, cut it out!'

It was a typical Adam short teaching session. The students had learned—and Lucy herself had been reminded of a few basics. She wondered if ever she would be a teacher herself.

She hadn't seen Gray for a few days. Lizzie's often sent staff to a number of outlying hospitals, and Gray had been asked to spend a week or so on a cancer ward in Lally's hospital, some miles away. He had phoned her on the ward to tell her where he was going, and that he'd decided to stay in the accommodation block in Lally's.

'There's a lot that has to be done here, Lucy. I need to live on the job.'

'Don't work too hard.'

She heard him chuckle. 'You say that to me? I could say the same but…hang on, there's my bleep. Bye, sweetheart, I'll be in touch.' He rang off.

He had called her sweetheart. She liked that.

Gary Priest was to be operated on the next day. It was Lucy's job to make all the arrangements, to see that there was a theatre ready, an anaesthetist available, blood cross-matched. Perhaps most important was obtaining the consent of Gary's parents.

Like so many parents, they were still in a state of shock. What had at first seemed to be a comparatively small problem had suddenly grown to a massive one. They had been reassured—the disease had been detected very early, it was still in stage one, there was no reason not to be reasonably optimistic. But they still could not take it on.

It was no use just asking for a signature. Lucy had been taught the parents must understand what was going to happen, must be made aware of the risks— even of the risks of an anaesthetic.

'The positive point is,' she said, 'we've caught the disease early. If we operate now we stand a good chance of halting it.'

'He's ever so small,' Mrs Priest said. 'Do you have to cut into him? I mean, can't he take drugs or something?'

'The consultant feels that this is by far the best way,' Lucy said. 'There's very little risk to surgery today.'

There was a pause, and then, 'Is it only a good chance?' Mr Priest said. 'You're not absolutely certain you can…can cure him?'

'No treatment is ever a hundred per cent certain. All I can say is, if I had a child, and he had this condition, this is what I would want.'

'But you haven't got a child,' Mrs Priest said. 'It's different, you know.'

In the end they signed. Lucy told them she would see them both the next day, and went just to sit down for five minutes. Some of her work was draining.

*   *   *

Gray rang her again three days later. This time the call came latish in the evening, when she had finished studying and was thinking of going to bed.

'Have you got five minutes?' he asked her. 'Not going out on one of your high-society adventures?'

A couple of weeks ago she would have bristled at the accusation, but she knew now that he was teasing her. 'A long line of men in dinner jackets are clamouring at my door,' she told him. 'Each is carrying a bottle of champagne and the car park outside is full of Rolls-Royces. But I'm staying in with my cocoa.'

'An excellent idea.' He paused a minute, and when he spoke again his voice was hesitant. 'In some ways I'm glad I'm talking to you by phone. Seeing you face to face would make things harder.'

What did he mean, 'harder'? Was he trying to get rid of her? Suddenly, the prospect of not seeing him, not hearing from him again was more than she could bear. But she managed to keep an even tone. 'Far be it from me to make things hard for you,' she said lightly.

'In some ways you already have. I came to England intending to study like a lunatic, to learn as much as I could so I could go back home and apply for my first consultant's job. I thought I didn't need any kind of social life. But I met you. And, in spite of all my good plans, I'm thinking of you far more than I ought.'

'Thank you for that tremendous testament to my charms,' she said. But he had made her heart beat faster; what he'd said had excited her. So she went on, 'I think of you a lot too, Gray.'

'Lucy, I phoned to say that I was thinking of you.

But there's also something else I must say. In five months I go back to Australia.'

There was nothing she could say to that. She knew it, of course. But somehow she managed to disregard the fact. 'I know,' she said. 'But I don't want to give up…I don't think it's necessary to…oh, hell, I still want to go on seeing you.'

'And I want to go on seeing you, very much. But I want to be fair to you. In five months I leave. So do we just keep on as we have been doing, see what develops, let the future take care of itself?'

'It's all we can do. And, don't forget, I've got my work too.'

He laughed. 'As if I could forget. Incidentally, have you heard from the police?'

'Yes, a sergeant phoned me. I've given them your address but basically I doubt you'll hear from them again. The lad is pleading guilty, there'll be no need for us to give evidence. He's in plenty of trouble already, we're only a small part of it.'

'Good. And what's-her-name…Judy Osmore…is she okay?'

'No great damage. In fact she's written asking if we can call round to see her some time when you're back. Do you know when that will be?'

'Not quite sure. The lady doctor whose place I am taking wants to come back as quickly as possible— in fact, I think she intends to disobey her doctor's orders. We can't approve of that. But with any luck I should be back quite late on Saturday.'

'I've got Sunday off. Gray, can we spend Sunday together? You've not seen much of England, I'd like to show you a bit. A special bit.'

She could tell he was intrigued. 'I'd like that. What special bit?'

She was still hesitant, not sure if she was doing right. But she wasn't going to tell him first. 'I want to keep it a secret. Till Sunday.'

'That suits me. Lucy…I think a lot of you.'

'I think a lot of you too,' she told him.

Early on Saturday afternoon she was sprawled on her bed, idly leafing through one of her textbooks. She was barefoot, dressed in old, easy clothes, having one of those all-too-rare hours when she had nothing much to do and was quite content to let time slide by. It didn't happen very often.

Someone knocked on her door, and she yelled, 'Come in.' Probably one of her friends from the block wanting to borrow her coffee, a stamp, perhaps a dress. Most of the girls there were of similar age—it often seemed as if she had fifty sisters to borrow from or lend to.

'I got off early, so I came straight to see you,' a male voice said. 'Have you missed me?'

It was Gray. She hadn't been expecting him till late that night. If he had come then, she would have been ready for him, expecting him, friendly but calm. As it was the sheer surprise made her heart pound and her breath catch in her throat. So she stood, and wordlessly hugged him. He kissed her, and she knew that…she knew that she would have to think about him again. She hadn't realised what an effect he could have on her.

Breathless, flushed, she eased from him. Like her, he was dressed casually, in jeans and sweater. And he looked so good! She didn't want to talk now about how much she had missed him, she wanted time to think.

'I wasn't expecting you till late this evening,' she accused.

'The lady I relieved was convinced I was doing something wrong,' came the amused reply. 'Perhaps taking over her work. She couldn't wait to get me out of her ward. We had a fifteen-minute handover, then it was made clear I was no longer needed.'

'She must have been…well, I'm glad you're here. D'you want a drink or something?'

He shook his head. 'I'm all full up of tea and coffee. If anything, I think I'd like some fresh air. I've seen nothing but the ward, the clinic and my bedroom for the past few days.'

'Come on, then,' she said, reaching for her socks, 'we'll walk round and see Judy Osmore.'

She had never really noticed the street where Judy Osmore had been attacked. It was a back street certainly, but it was an affluent one. There was a row of specialist shops, one specialising in leather furniture, one an up-market travel shop, one selling antiquarian books. The shop Judy Osmore had left was called simply 'Judy's Boutique'. Across the top of the window and down one side there were painted pictures of Punch and Judy. In the window itself there was a handful of dresses. Lucy saw at a glance that they were expensive ones.

They walked in the shop. There was subdued lighting, quiet background music, a thick carpet. The dresses on show were scattered artfully around the shop; there was no crowding of models.

'Drs Brett and Woods! How lovely of you to come!'

The woman who came towards them from the back of the shop was vastly different from the sobbing creature they had rescued the week before. Judy Osmore was dressed expensively in black, her hair carefully arranged. She made Lucy feel out of place in her trainers and old clothes.

'How are you, Mrs Osmore?' Gray asked. 'No long-term ill effects, I hope?'

'Not really. In many ways it was a valuable lesson. The police have been round and showed me how to improve security, there's a firm going to fetch the money in future. I was just being stupid. Now, I was about to have a glass of China tea, would you like to join me?'

She ushered them into a back room, and poured three tiny glasses of aromatic tea. It was a while since Lucy had drunk it; she'd forgotten how refreshing it was.

Under the stronger light she could see Mrs Osmore's face more clearly. There was a great bruise on her cheek, the darkness cleverly hidden by pancake make-up.

'You were very lucky,' she said. 'If he had hit you much harder he might have broken your cheek-bone. Reconstruction would have taken quite a while.'

'Well, I certainly wasn't going to give up my hard-earned cash without a fight. But fortunately you two came along, and things worked out not too badly.'

She turned to an antique chest of drawers and took a parcel from it. It was expensively, professionally wrapped in dark red shiny paper. She offered the parcel to Gray.

'Now, I hope I'm not going to have any trouble with you two,' she said. 'Dr Gray, I told my husband your colouring and together we picked these for you. A very small token of our gratitude.'

Gray looked embarrassed. 'Mrs Osmore, we're both doctors, we can't accept presents from...'

'You weren't doctors when you helped me, you were passers-by on the way for a drink. Now please open it and tell me if we've picked well. My husband says that no woman should pick a tie, so he helped me.'

Silently Gray opened the package. Inside were half a dozen silk ties, three in sombre colours, three in rich.

'What do you think of them, Dr Brett?' Mrs Osmore asked. 'Shouldn't he keep them?'

'They're gorgeous,' Lucy agreed cheerfully. 'They make me wish I was a man, just for once.'

'That's settled, then. Dr Woods, have some more tea, I'm taking Dr Brett into our changing room.'

'But I didn't...' protested Lucy, guessing what was coming, but it was to no avail. She was whisked into the main salon, and eyed with that assessing pursed-lip look that she had seen in so many saleswomen.

'Size, a tall twelve, perhaps fourteen,' Mrs Osmore muttered, 'dark colouring so we echo it or add to it...'

Lucy felt she had to say something. 'Look, I didn't do anything. Gray chased the man. All I did was...'

'You comforted me,' Mrs Osmore said simply, 'and I needed it so much. Not every doctor realises that. I gather you're still training, but one day you'll be a simply splendid doctor. Now get out of that appalling green garment you're wearing and I'll see what I have in stock.'

Lucy sighed and did as she was told.

Mrs Osmore brought five dresses, and Lucy tried

them all on. But in the end there was one obvious choice. A sleeveless blue cocktail dress in a midnight blue so dark as to be almost black. The cut was apparently simple, but it was the simplicity that concealed art. 'It'll hang better when you're wearing a slip,' Mrs Osmore said. 'Silk always does. And those white socks don't add much to the overall effect. But go and see what your boyfriend thinks of it.'

'He's not really my boyfriend,' Lucy said. 'Well, perhaps he will be, but not quite yet.'

'Show him that dress and he'll make his mind up quickly.'

Mrs Osmore was right. Gray looked stunned when he saw her. 'You look beautiful,' he said hoarsely.

Lucy turned to Mrs Osmore. 'Yes, if you're absolutely sure, I would like it,' she said.

Five minutes later she and Gray were walking back towards the hospital, each happily clutching a parcel. 'I still feel a bit uneasy,' she said. 'I don't like people feeling that they have to give me something.'

'She didn't feel that she had to give you something. She felt that she wanted to. Sometimes people need to show gratitude.'

'All right, I'll remember that. Now, you're all right for a mystery trip tomorrow morning, starting early?'

'Looking forward to it.'

'Then let's go and have a pizza or something and have an early night.'

It was just getting light when they met next morning. He was dressed as she had told him to, in comfortable sweater and jeans, an anorak over his arm and light boots on his feet. She was dressed similarly. It was only a few hours since she had seen him but she still got a thrill when he first walked out of the door. He looked good whatever he wore!

'Have you brought a camera?' she asked, suddenly aware that she had forgotten her own.

'I've brought a camera, in case we go sightseeing. Is this your car? I might have guessed you wouldn't have an ordinary saloon.'

In fact she didn't drive much at all in the centre of London. But she had bought a maroon Vitara, thinking that it was best to have something small in London, and she liked the extra height that the car gave her. And, after driving on the rough tracks of the American north-west, she had grown accustomed to the extra margin of safety given by the four-wheel drive.

'This does me very well. As they say, it's neat but not gaudy. Climb aboard.'

They swung out of the car park and onto the main road. Because it was Sunday there wasn't an awful lot of traffic about and she expertly threaded her way through the centre. 'Not worried about being driven by a woman driver?' she asked half challengingly.

He didn't answer as she decisively overtook a lorry that was happily straddling two lanes. Then, 'I'm certainly not worried being driven by you. I knew you'd be competent. You seem to be competent at everything you do.'

'Just wait till you know me better,' she told him. But the compliment pleased her.

It didn't take them too long to get out of London, and soon they were on the M40. There were green fields now; they were approaching real country. High Wycombe flashed past on their right, and the traffic grew less dense.

They talked easily about medical matters, cases she was interested in, and his views of the latest drugs. He told her a little about working in Australia, what it was like to inhabit a continent with so few people. It was a pleasant conversation, but one in which neither gave much away. She thought that they had been too intense recently, they needed some kind of space. But she knew this couldn't last. This trip she had organised would see to that. She hoped she was doing right.

They bypassed Oxford. He turned to her, half surprised. 'Somehow I thought you were taking me there,' he said. 'It seemed to be an obvious destination. Surely we're not going to Birmingham?'

'Not Birmingham,' she said. 'Somewhere more interesting—to you.'

'Now that is an enigmatic remark.' But he didn't ask her for further details.

She turned right off the motorway and into an area of gentle hills and tiny villages. The motorway was quickly forgotten; this land had not changed much in centuries. She had memorised the map before she set off, and followed the twisting roads and intersections expertly.

'You obviously know your way,' he said.

'No. I've never been here before in my life.' Soon they would be at their destination. It was time to prepare him a little. She hoped things would be all right.

'I'm not going to be defensive,' she said, 'but people have always been interested in our family history. I told you we never seem to throw any records away, people—historians—are always writing asking if they can look through the archives, read letters and so on. Well, we had a young researcher come a couple of months ago. George Timmons, from London University. Perhaps we helped him more than people usually did—at any rate, he was very grateful and said if ever he could help us, he would.' She paused, not quite certain what to say next.

'Go on.' His voice was still pleasant, but she wondered if she could detect a touch of iron in it. He knew she had planned something for him and she was now uneasy, knowing that she was risking his anger.

'Well, I phoned him last week, asked him to do a bit of research for me. Always ask an expert if you can. And he told me that a lot of records are now computerised, easy to get at if you know where to look.'

'You're rambling, Lucy. Get to the point.'

'I'm trying to. It's hard.'

They passed through Anerton, a village of golden stone with thatched cottages. 'The next village is Setchell,' she said. 'That's where we are going. There's a fine old church there, St George's. In the churchyard are three graves with Woods on the headstones. They're your ancestors, Gray. I got George Timmons to trace them.'

He said nothing. For a moment she took her eyes off the twisting road; his face looked distant, remote. When she could stand the silence no longer she muttered, 'I hope you're not angry with me.'

For what seemed like an eternity, he didn't reply. Then, 'No,' he said. 'But it is a shock.'

They reached Setchell. It was a larger village than many they had passed through, with newer houses on the outskirts. The centre looked older. There was a square with an old market cross, a black and white half-timbered pub. To one side, on a little rise, they could see the high steeple of the flint stone church.

She pulled into a parking place and Gray climbed out and looked round, silently. Obviously he was still slightly shocked. Lucy felt she had come so far, she might as well carry on. Taking an envelope from her bag, she said, 'This is all the paperwork George has sent me so far. If you want we can throw it into the bin, and just walk away.'

He smiled, though it seemed strained. 'I've never walked away from anything in my life,' he said. 'But this certainly feels very odd. How can I be so…doubtful about what you've done? I've just realised how different having a background can make you feel. Up to now I've thought having a family like yours was—well, vaguely comic. But now I can see—or feel—the point of it.'

'You bought me a brandy last week when I was a bit shaken up,' she said. 'Shall I buy you one now, in that pub? You can look through these papers, and then go to the churchyard—if you want.'

He grinned at her. 'You're doing an SHO's job. All the paperwork, preliminary investigations, permission from the patient's parents, tentative diagnosis, then let the registrar look. I don't need a brandy, but we could go to the pub for a coffee if you like.'

'I'd like that.' They set off across the square.

As they entered the pub—The Shelton Arms—she pointed to a date carved into the lintel. 1749. 'Your ancestors might have drunk here,' she told him, 'and they probably got married in the church.'

A haunted look passed over his face. 'It seems strange to think that,' he said. 'And then transported from here to Australia. What a difference!'

They found a pleasant front room, not too busy. She smiled to herself when he accepted her offer to order the coffee; it wasn't like him. He obviously wanted to start looking through the papers at once. He had them spread out on the table, and moved them only reluctantly when the coffee tray arrived.

'This man George Timmons is quite an impressive researcher,' he said, obviously fascinated. 'He's indicated where he can go for further information if we need it. He's even phoned to find exactly where the graves are.'

Lucy poured two coffees. 'He also says that it might be possible to trace vague relations who are still alive. Would you like that?'

'I'm not sure,' he said after a pause. 'This is all too new. Once you've found relations then they're yours, you can't get rid of them. Like them or not, you have to live with the knowledge that they are there.'

'Welcome to the real world,' she told him cheerfully. 'Don't forget there's one or two of my ancestors I'm not too happy about. We were landowners and JPs. Do you realise they might have sentenced people to transportation?'

'Now there's a thought.' He shuffled the papers into a neat pile, and slid them carefully into the envelope.

Quite deliberately he changed the conversation. He told her how much he enjoyed English pubs, how there was nothing quite like them in Australia. This one, The Shelton Arms, was really comfortable. Again, she knew he was deliberately putting off talking to her about what she had done. That was fine. She could imagine the shock.

After they had finished the coffee they walked across the square and into the churchyard. They walked through a newer section, with bright white and polished black stones. Many of the graves had flowers on them. Round the back of the church was the older section. The grass was still cut, but the headstones were of old grey stone, covered in green lichen. Many were at an angle; some had fallen.

He had remembered the instructions, and led her straight to the three Woods graves. She opened the box of tissues she had brought for the purpose, and rubbed away the lichen. The names were there.

He stood transfixed, so after a while she left him and went to sit on a bench by the side of the church. Then he came and sat by her, put his arm round her shoulders and hugged and kissed her, in a completely non-sexual way.

'I want to thank you for bringing me here,' he said. 'It's affected me more than I thought; my life is different from what it was this morning.'

'What d'you want to do now?' she asked.

'I want to walk round this village. There must be bits of it that my ancestors saw. I want to see them too. Then we'll come back here and I want to take some photographs, go inside the church.'

'So are you going to ask George to trace your family?'

'I think I am,' he said, 'in time.'

'You can go home tomorrow, Sam,' Lucy said to the fifteen-year-old. 'Your parents will fetch you and they've got your bedroom ready.'

'Great,' Sam Westby said wearily. 'Will I still feel so knackered, Lucy?'

'I know the treatment is a bit hard,' she said. 'But it's working. You'll get your strength back over the next few weeks. And in a couple of months you'll be as good as new. Now, let's have a look in your mouth.'

He opened obediently. Patients sometimes developed unpleasant ulcers after the treatment, and Lucy and the nurses had been at pains to teach Sam how to keep his mouth free from infection.

'Very good,' she said approvingly. And indeed it was. Sam had been a model patient, doing everything he had been told. 'Now, you know we've not finished with you yet. We want to see you at our clinic. I'll give your mother a card.'

'Thanks, Lucy. Er…will I see you again?'

'I'll make a point of coming down to the clinic,' she promised him.

As she walked back down the ward, she felt elated. They had caught Sam's disease in time, they had saved him from suffering and almost certain death. Sometimes, being a cancer doctor wasn't too bad.

She was sitting in the doctors' room, just finishing the last of the reports on her desk, when the door opened.

'That's what I like to see,' said Gray cheerfully. 'The lower orders carrying on happily with their humble chores.'

She scowled at him. 'If you know any treatment for a numb backside, then I'd like to hear about it. These hospital chairs are an instrument of torture. And I think I've got writer's cramp too.'

He came in and sat down. 'Make me a coffee and I'll do a bit of the paperwork. Stand up, touch your toes, stretch your back, loosen your spine. You'll feel better once the blood is flowing.'

'A PT instructor as well as a doctor and a masseur,' she said, but doing as he had recommended. 'You know, I do feel better.'

'Human beings weren't designed to sit for long periods,' he told her. 'Running or lying is better.'

'Unfortunately both those make it rather difficult to write. Anyhow, what are you doing here? I thought you had a clinic.'

'I did have, we finished early. I came to tell you I've received an invitation to dinner from your father. For next Saturday.'

She was delighted. 'Good! You are going to accept?'

'Since you're going to be there, of course. Tell me a bit about what to expect.'

She pulled a face. 'I don't go so often now because I'm usually working. But when I do go, I always enjoy myself. His parties are famous—or infamous. He won't have anyone there unless he actually wants to talk to them. Not like House affairs, where he says there are too many bores.'

'House affairs?'

'Er, House of Lords,' she mumbled. 'He has to do a lot of entertaining.' Then she rushed on, 'But he likes a bit of formality at his own dinners, so they're always black tie. I'll wear a longish dress.'

'And you can invite anyone you wish?'

'Well, sort of. But my brothers would tell me off afterwards if I brought along what they'd call a right prat.'

'So this is a kind of vote of confidence in me? A decision that I'm not a prat?'

'I've got every confidence in your non-pratfulness,' she said. 'Shall we share a taxi to get there?'

'I'll pick you up at your room.'

CHAPTER SIX

LUCY always thought that evening wear enhanced a man, and Gray certainly looked well in his. The pure white of his shirt was set off by the remains of his tan, not yet extinguished by the English weather. His well-cut suit emphasised the fact that he was an athlete. 'You look well,' she told him.

'Not as well as you,' he replied softly.

She had on a yellow calf-length dress in linen, with a pleated, swirling skirt and a tighter top. 'Thank you, sir,' she said, pirouetting so the skirt billowed round her. 'Let's say we make a handsome couple.'

Their taxi was waiting. 'Tell me about your family,' he said as they settled themselves inside. 'I feel like a suitor going to meet the future in-laws so they can decide if he is good enough for their daughter.'

'If you were a suitor,' she said firmly, 'then I can assure you that the daughter would decide for herself. But this is not that kind of occasion. To give him his full title, my father is the Earl of Bellings. He's a hereditary peer, but is much respected for the work he's done. He's a Government spokesman on the environment. He doesn't bother about his title too much himself, he's more proud of his army DSM.'

'The DSM? You get that for bravery. Where and why did he get it?' Gray was obviously impressed.

'Somewhere in the Arabian Peninsula,' she said. 'He doesn't talk about it so I don't know very much. Now I've also got two older brothers. James is a

Cambridge Fellow, an economist, and he's always advising the Government on how to spend money. The youngest of my brothers, Michael, does something in the City and makes lots of money. He speaks perfect Chinese and Japanese.'

'And your mother?

'She died having me. It was HELLP syndrome—you know—a complication of pregnancy-induced hypertension. She wouldn't have died today. I was brought up by my father.'

'And he never remarried?'

'He never even thought of it. He says he was happy with a woman once, he couldn't imagine being so happy again. That's the kind of love I want some day.'

'I see,' he said, and she blushed. He went on, 'So he brought you up. I suppose you went to an upper-class boarding-school.'

'Certainly not! We had a home, all three of us stayed there.'

He thought for a while. 'From what you tell me of them, I guess both your brothers did very well at school. And you were the youngest. What was it like coming after those two?'

'It was hard,' she admitted. 'But the pressure came from me, not from anyone else. When I was eighteen I just didn't know what to do, so I went walkabout for five years. Then I decided I wanted to be a doctor. And before you ask, I never once mentioned any of my family when I was applying for medical school.'

He looked at her expressionlessly. 'My ideas about you are changing, young Brett. That idea never even crossed my mind. And I'm looking forward to meeting your family. They sound like what I would have expected.'

What did he mean by that? she asked herself.

They arrived a little early—she wanted to introduce Gray to her father and brothers before the other guests arrived. She watched as they tried to make him feel welcome, and then questioned him on the difference between the Australian and British health services. It was a typical conversation for her family, and she could see how Gray was enjoying himself.

The other guests came an hour later. There was a TV journalist, a female American economist, another lady who had done well starting her own software company, a someone in the City and the owner of a small fleet of oil tankers. In fact, a typical group at her father's table.

Dinner was served almost at once. As usual the meal was excellent but light; people came for the conversation not the gourmandising. The wine too was excellent but everyone drank in moderation. The butler deftly served, and Lucy settled herself to listen, and occasionally take part.

The topic quickly seized on was how to improve and pay for the National Health Service. Gray pointed out that, with modern developments, research needed a bottomless money supply. He also explained how, when he'd been working in the USA, he had been told to insist that paying patients take every possible test, necessary or not. This was to avoid the chance of future litigation. The people round the table wondered if this attitude would come to Britain soon.

It was an interesting evening, and as ever it broke up early. Lucy heard her father inviting Gray to lunch at the House, there were a couple of people there who would like to hear what he had to say. 'You're not planning on staying in this country, then?' he asked.

'I'm afraid not. I shall return to Australia in about four months.'

'I think that's a pity, we need people like you in the health service. But you must make up your own mind.'

Soon she was again in a taxi with Gray. 'Did you enjoy yourself?' she asked.

'Very much so. Everyone there was a money man—or woman—and that's not the kind of person I normally enjoy meeting. But now I know more about what they do, I'm impressed.'

'So do you still think I'm a mindless social butterfly?'

'Nope. Now I think you're an intelligent social butterfly. Ow!'

'I'm a butterfly with a hard fist,' she said cheerfully. 'When I was younger I used to punch my brothers when they teased me. I hope I didn't hurt you.'

'Not at all. I was once kicked in the chest by a kangaroo. It felt very similar. Now, I checked, your next shift is lates on Monday. Would you like to take a thirty-six-hour break with me, starting early tomorrow morning? Say seven o'clock?'

Her heart beat faster when he said thirty-six hours. What had he in mind? 'We'll be away overnight?' she asked cautiously.

'Of course we will. But we'll be in separate rooms in a hotel, nothing crass, Lady Lucy.'

'Where are we going?'

'You took me on a mystery ride last week. Now I

want to do the same for you. I'd like to start off in your car, but only for half an hour or so.'

Stranger and stranger. 'All right,' she said, 'I like surprises. What shall I bring?'

'Wear the same as last week. Warmish clothes, a pair of boots or strong shoes. But bring something for the evening. Something like the dress you're wearing.'

'Easily done.' The taxi pulled up outside the block of flats, and they stepped out and headed towards them. Halfway to the door there was a convenient patch of darkness. He stopped, pulled her to him. His kiss was passionate, demanding, and she allowed herself to sink towards him, her mouth soft beneath his, her body yielding under his caresses. She could feel his eagerness for her, and she wanted him. 'Do you want to come up for cocoa or something?' she asked.

He shook his head. 'I want to. But not tonight. It might not be a good idea.'

'Till tomorrow morning, then?'

'Till tomorrow morning.'

He kissed her again quickly on the stairs before they parted, and whispered, 'I'll call for you at seven, then.' Immediately she ran up the next flight of stairs, leaving him behind. She knew that if she stopped a minute longer then she would have to invite him back with her. And she knew he would come.

He didn't follow her. She entered her friendly little room on autopilot, without thinking, doing the things that she always did. She hung up her dress, cleaned her face with cream, showered, brushed her teeth, fetched the regulation mug of cocoa. Then she sat on her bed, hugging her knees. It couldn't be put off any longer. She had to think. What were her feelings for Gray Woods?

To start with she had dealt with him in the friendly but brisk fashion with which she dealt with so many of the men in her life. Years of being alone and on the road had taught her how to get on with men, neither offending them nor suggesting that there was anything sexual in her offers of friendship. She knew she was adept at this. It had angered her when Gray had misunderstood her, thought she was not serious about her job. She had quickly put him right. They had had a couple of meetings, she got on well with him, when he kissed her she liked it.

So far he had not been too different from men she had met before. They had been friends—sometimes quite close friends—but never in any sense lovers. And in general she thought it best not to get involved emotionally with men she worked with closely. But she was letting Gray get to her. He was beginning to affect her.

The trip to find his ancestors' graves had started almost as half a joke, to prove to him that really he was no different from her. But she had become as fascinated as he was. She had invited Gray to dinner with her father—something she had never done with any other man. Kenneth Copley had heard about the occasions, had dropped broad hints that he would like an invitation. She had ignored the hints.

What did Gray think of her? What were his plans for her—if any? He had been absolutely straight with her—in four months he would go back to Australia. She could sympathise with his absolute dedication—it was a trait she had met before in her own family. She thought he was losing his vague prejudice about her being 'upper class'; he was too intelligent to hold that against her. So…?

So far her thoughts had been almost at random, now she had to face up to the hard question. For the first time in her life, was she truly, really, absolutely in love? Her mind shied away from the question; she made herself face up to it. She realised there was no one she could ask for advice. All the other girls and women in the hospital accommodation block were constantly debating their love life, asking advice. She could do neither.

Through the years in school, warily comparing her performance with that of her brothers, through the five years' wandering the planet and the six years' medical training, she had developed a toughness, an ability to be self-contained. Now she desperately needed advice, she didn't know how to ask for it. And she couldn't decide what she wanted herself.

She sighed, drained her cocoa and climbed under the duvet. She couldn't sleep. This was ridiculous; she could always sleep. All junior doctors slept the minute they had chance, it was part of the job description. But not this time.

After ten minutes' heaving about the bed, she got up again. There was no way she could study, so she packed a bag with the outdoor clothes prescribed by Gray, and, after some thought, added the blue dress given by Judy Osmore. Perhaps the realisation that she was packing for time to be spent with Gray calmed her. When she went back to bed she slept at once.

'Drive north,' he said. 'Get on the M1 and I'll direct you from there. We'll turn off after about fifteen minutes.'

'Are you going to tell me where we're going?' She was curious.

'This is my revenge,' he said with some satisfaction. 'I want it to be a surprise, like you gave me with my ancestors. Incidentally, this has got nothing to do with them.'

'That was the first thing I wondered,' she said. 'So tell me, what d'you think about having a family now?'

His hand was resting on the dashboard, and she heard his fingers drum on the plastic—the first sign of nerves she'd ever seen in him. 'I've been in touch with the archivist, George Timmons. He is a nice chap. I've asked him to trace if there are any of my relations left alive. If there are—I'll go to see them.'

She thought about this for a moment, and then said, 'You must be under some strain, then—there's a lot of tension in waiting.'

'Some. But I'm going back to Australia soon. If there are any problems I shall leave them behind me.'

She realised this wasn't the answer she'd wanted to hear.

They were now out of built-up London; there was the odd green field to be seen. He told her to take the next turn-off, along a main highway and then onto a narrower road. They were among fields again, and ahead she saw the bright orange of a wind-sock. There must be a flying club near here. She came up to the entrance, and to her surprise he told her to turn in. There was the usual couple of hangars, a scattering of smaller buildings and a handful of brightly coloured little planes.

'What are we doing here?' she asked in surprise. 'You're not taking me flying?'

'I certainly am,' he said cheerfully. 'You must have flown in one of these before?'

'Yes, quite a bit in America. But do you have a pilot's licence?'

'In Australia I needed one. I told you before, although most of our patients live reasonably handy, there are quite a few who still live in the outback. I like to keep an eye on those who are in remission, and often it's a lot of grief for them to have to come into hospital just for half a day. So I fly out to see them. I often can see two or three in one trip. I could have a pilot, of course, but I decided to learn to fly and now I really enjoy it. It's the obvious thing to do.'

She thought about this a moment. Then, 'No, it isn't,' she said. 'It would be more economic for them to come to you. You just fly out to spare them, don't you?'

'Well, just a little,' he said.

Apparently he had been to the little airfield before; he was greeted warmly in the office. It reminded her just a bit of hospital—whatever you had to do there were a thousand forms to fill in first. So she sat in the little lounge, surrounded by pictures of ancient planes, and read a flying magazine as he talked and signed. There was the roar of an engine overhead. Then he came to her and said, 'I've filed a flight plan, let's go.'

She was given a helmet to wear, walked with him across the tarmac to where a little maroon plane was waiting, its propeller already noisily whirling. It all came back to her, though she hadn't flown in one of

these for over six years. She climbed into the little
cockpit and watched him climb in beside her. Twin
sets of controls faced them. Her door was slammed
shut.

She didn't speak as he went through the usual set
of pre-flight checks, but after he radioed the tower
and asked for permission for take-off, she said, 'This
is really exciting. I always seem to be doing exciting
things with you.'

He looked at her sardonically. 'We'll have to keep
that up,' he said, and she blushed.

There was a louder snarl of the engine, and they
taxied down to the far side of the field where he
checked with the control tower again. Then they were
bumping, ever faster, down the long strip of grass in
front of them.

She had forgotten how slow little planes were,
compared to the great jets that hurried her across con-
tinents. But this take-off was far more fun. There was
a bouncy start, a greater impression of speed, and then
the little machine seemed to haul itself into the air.
Yes, it was fun.

Gray was engrossed with his work so she looked
at him happily. There was the same calm air, easy
confidence that she had seen on the ward, in the
theatre. His hands were big and looked strong, but
she knew them capable of such delicacy. They rested
on the yoke, making easy adjustments as his eyes
flicked from control panel to horizon. His body
seemed perfectly relaxed, there was none of the tension she had seen in other, sometimes very competent,
pilots.

She felt a great rush of...what? She didn't know
exactly what emotion. There was excitement cer-

tainly, but also affection. Was it more than that? She knew she would shortly have to examine her feelings again. But for the moment she was going to enjoy herself.

Looking out of the window she could see tiny houses flitting past, the silver curl of a river, what seemed like toy smoke from a factory. She felt so exhilarated, to be here in the air, with this man. Impulsively, she leaned over, kissed him on the cheek. 'This is wonderful,' she shouted above the noise of the engine. 'Thank you so much for bringing me. There's so much room up here in the air—look at that crowded road below.'

He grinned. 'This sky is crowded compared with Australia. But I like flying. It's safe, just so long as you remain in control.'

He reached over, took one of her hands and squeezed. 'I like doing things with you, Lucy. You're an enthusiast. You say you've flown in small planes before?'

'Just a bit. In the north-west of America.'

'Want to take the controls a minute? I'll bet you've tried before.'

Of course, he was right. She put her hands firmly on the juddering yoke in front of her. 'Taking over,' she said. Gently she dived, climbed and banked, the little plane throbbing under her hands, responsive to her wishes. It felt good. Then she handed control back to him. 'Thank you,' she said, 'that was fun. Now are you going to tell me where we're going or are you keeping it a secret?'

'Ah. I fancied a bit of fresh air. We've been too long in the hospital. I love London, but we've been there too long without seeing much of the rest of the country.'

'I could show you more,' she said.

'You know me. I'm here to work, not wander round like a tourist.'

There it was again, that absolute dedication. She respected it, but at times it frightened her.

'Anyway,' he went on, 'we're going up to the north Yorkshire coast. Two reasons. I was up country once, a searing hot day, to see a lad who was in remission from leukaemia. In fact he was doing rather well. I talked to his dad who said he loved the country, but just occasionally he missed his home town. Just now and then he'd like a bit of chill, a bit of rain. He came from Scarborough. So I thought I'd like to come and see it.'

'Very believable,' she said. 'And the second reason?'

For a moment she almost thought he looked shame-faced. 'I guess I'm just a little boy at heart. I want to travel on a steam train. There's a place near Scarborough called Pickering. It has steam trains that run up into the Yorkshire Dales. I want to go on one.'

'You're an idiot,' she told him affectionately. 'Imagine coming halfway across the world to travel on a train. But I must say, I rather fancy it myself.'

They landed about midday, on another small air-field very similar to the one they'd taken off from. The landing should have been exciting; as ever he managed it calmly and efficiently. A mechanic took the plane away, said he would have it ready for them tomorrow. 'You only pay for the time you have it in the air,' Gray commented. 'They have the same system in Australia.'

A quick visit to the office and then they walked out to where a hired car was waiting for them. For a moment they both stood before getting in. 'The air smells different here,' she said. 'Damper and more—countrified. I think I'm going to enjoy myself.'

'Come on,' he said, 'we've time for a sandwich before the train is due. I've got a map and timetables here.'

She enjoyed the trip on the train. She wouldn't have thought so, but the noise, the old-fashioned carriages, above all the smells of steam and smoke—all were intensely evocative. The countryside was attractive too. It was fun watching the clouds of steam puff away across the bleak moorland. Of course, it didn't have the sheer size of the north of America, but it was attractive all the same.

The train was crowded; there were lots of tourists and train enthusiasts. She was pushed against him; she quite liked it. When they reached their destination they walked a while round the little grey-stone village. Unashamedly, she held his hand. 'I'm glad you brought me here,' she said. 'It's helping me to relax, untying a few knots. Sometimes you just don't realise how stressed you are.'

He agreed with her. 'It's a big danger in hospital. Sometimes you get hooked on it, start to thrive on the constant excitement. You live on adrenaline. That's when you're likely to make a mistake. You need to force yourself to slow down, even though you don't think it necessary.'

'Have you ever made a mistake? Don't tell me if you don't want.'

'Never a big mistake—or at least never one that I couldn't put right. And I don't mind telling you, it's important that you hear about mistakes as well as about successes. The biggest mistake I did make was when I'd been up for twenty-seven hours and I wrote a hundred mils on a prescription instead of ten mils. Fortunately the nurse with me questioned what I had done. I made myself go for a sleep at once.'

'I see,' she said thoughtfully. 'That's interesting.'

The trip back was equally enjoyable, but it was getting dark when they reached Pickering again and climbed back in the hire car. 'What now?' she asked. She felt curious and just a touch apprehensive, she didn't know why.

'To the hotel, I think. It's a big one, perhaps a bit old-fashioned but with a reputation for good food. I'm sure you'll like it. It's only about half an hour's drive from here. We can have a warm drink first if you wish.'

He was responsive to the slightest change in her mood. She shook her head. 'I'm fine. Let's get to the hotel and see how things are there.'

It was typical of him that he had studied the map well in advance. He drove unerringly through dark-ened fields and little villages, and then into the neon-lit outskirts of the coastal town. Scarborough itself was surprisingly hilly, but he twisted through the little streets and eventually they arrived at the front of a vast building.

By now she was half asleep; the combination of fresh air and new surroundings had quite tired her. Their bags were taken up and the car driven round to the rear garage. Lucy sat in the ornate foyer as Gray booked them in and then escorted her to her room. 'You're hungry,' he said. 'You need blood sugar.

Change for dinner and I'll call for you in about half an hour.'

'Don't worry, I'll be ready. I'm a junior doctor, remember. We don't need sleep.'

'Half an hour, then. I'm only just down the corridor in Room 417.' He left her to look round her room.

The first thing she noticed was the coffee/tea-making tray, and the large pile of biscuits. She ate three chocolate digestives, told herself that she didn't want to spoil her dinner, but felt much better for it. Then she looked round her room with a more alert eye.

It was an old-fashioned room, skilfully modernised. The high ceilings, mahogany furniture, big double bed remained. In one corner was a door to an ornate bathroom, and she decided to have a bath rather than a shower. For once she would indulge herself. She bathed, washed her hair and took the drier out of her bag, which had been left by the bed. After four minutes in front of the large mirror, she pulled her dressing gown closer round her and decided to look out of the window. Full-length red curtains fell down one corner of the room. She peered through the curtains—and was entranced.

There were well-fitting French windows leading to a balcony. She opened the windows and stepped out. Before she hadn't noticed, but the hotel stood high on a hill. Below her there was the curve of a bay, lights dotted along the promenade and out by the harbour. Opposite her there was a floodlit castle perched on top of a wooded hill. And beyond was the darkest blue of the sea. She gasped with pleasure, it was so beautiful.

She had to phone him. 'You're at the back of the

hotel, you haven't got a view like mine. Gray, it's beautiful!'

He sounded amused. 'I'm quite happy with what I do have. There's a high hill here, it says it's called Oliver's Mount.'

'Well, I think you've cheated yourself. I want you to come and look at my view, just sit and enjoy it. There's nothing like this in London.'

'Shall I come now?'

'Good Lord, no. I've got another ten minutes, haven't I?'

'Not a second longer. I'm beginning to get hungry.'

She was not like many women she knew—even for a special occasion she was accustomed to dressing quickly. Since she was going to wear her new dress for the first time, she had packed the new underwear she had bought to go with it. She believed implicitly in the axiom that you dressed well from the inside out. An expensive dress needed and deserved expensive undies.

She pulled on lacy white briefs, a white bra so soft she barely knew it was there. A silk slip in dark blue to match the dress. For once she wouldn't bother with tights. But she had a good pair of black leather shoes. A little more make-up than usual, but not too much, a last quick brush of the hair. Then she was ready. She turned slowly in front of the full-length mirror. She had to admit it. She looked good!

There was a knock at the door and her heart started to beat wildly. Why? She knew who it was, she'd spent all day with him, she was expecting him. Her heart beat anyway.

He had looked well in sweater, boots and jeans. He looked even better in his dark suit, with white shirt and rich coloured silk tie. Taking her forearms in his hands, he leaned forward to kiss her gently on the mouth. 'You look so wonderful,' he muttered. 'That dress from Judy Osmore's—it might have been made…it does so much for you.'

'And you're a fitting partner,' she said lightly, 'but, yes, it is a lovely dress. Now are we…?'

She frowned at him questioningly as there was another knock at the door. 'Are we…?'

'There's a while before dinner. I thought we might look at this view of yours in some style.' He opened the door to a waiter, who pushed in a trolley bearing a bottle in an ice bucket, two glasses, a plate of nuts and petits fours. He wheeled the trolley to an occasional table, carefully popped the cork and poured two glasses of sparkling white wine. As he left, Gray took a glass and handed it to her. 'To us,' he said.

The wine was sharp, biscuity, instantly stimulating. The bubbles fizzed in her mouth. She knew her wines, and this was a good one—in fact, she thought it was the best she had ever tasted! 'This is glorious! What is it?' she gasped.

'Sorry, I'm being a bit chauvinistic. It's not real champagne, it's an Australian sparkling wine from Margaret River. But I like it.'

'I think it's wonderful.' She sipped again. 'But now it's time for my surprise.'

She stepped over to the curtains, pulled them back with a flourish. If anything, the view was even better than ten minutes ago. The moon had risen, there was its white globe in the sky, and the waves were dappled with silver. Both of them stood in silence for a minute.

'You organised the moon on purpose, didn't you?'

she asked him. 'Just to make this absolutely and altogether romantic.'

'All part of the service,' he agreed. 'And it is truly beautiful.' He opened the French windows and together they stepped onto the balcony. It was even more wonderful in the open air. For a moment she didn't register the cold, just the beauty of her surroundings.

They stood silent now, sipping their drinks. It seemed natural that he should stand behind her, put his glass down and lean both his arms over her shoulders, pull her back against him. He kissed her on the side of her head, on her hair. She said nothing, watching the moonlight on the water.

She shivered. 'You're cold,' he said, instantly solicitous. 'We'd better get back inside.'

'In a minute,' she said. He didn't realise that the shiver was one of excitement, of anticipation, rather than one of cold. But he moved her back inside anyway. Perhaps it was better that he did.

'There's lipstick on your face,' she said prosaically when they were back in her room. 'Here, lean forward and I'll wipe it away.' She dabbed at him with a cleaning tissue. 'Now, are we going down for dinner?'

'Of course. Shall we come back and finish the bottle later?' Anticipation thrilled through her body again.

She knew that the dinner was good but, although she ate, she hardly tasted anything. They ate lightly grilled fish caught that afternoon, with grilled vegetables and afterwards cheese. Knowing that there was a bottle waiting for them upstairs, they just had a glass of white wine with the fish, and a red with the cheese.

She knew that she should be paying more attention to her surroundings, to the ornamented dining room, to the unobtrusive service, to the perfectly cooked and prepared food. But she had eyes only for the man with her. He seemed the same, though in the past she had noticed that he was a man with a hearty appetite—like her own.

They said little during the meal. But they looked at each other, and she felt that she knew what he was thinking.

Eventually the meal was over, the waiter looking reproachfully at their hardly touched cheese. 'Coffee?' Gray asked.

'Let's make it in my room later,' she suggested. 'There's a kettle, lots of little packets. But there's your wine first.' They rose to leave.

In her bedroom she switched on one bedside light, and turned the rest off, so the room was in semi-darkness. Then she pulled back the curtains, opened the French windows, dragged a couch to where they could sit and gaze. The moon was higher now, silvering the entire sea below them.

'Sit by me,' she asked softly. 'We can look at the moon and the sea together.' But suddenly, he seemed restless. He had poured them another glass of wine each, and he walked outside with his, leaned over the balcony, then came inside and wandered aimlessly round her room. 'All this movement, you're making me dizzy,' she complained mildly. 'What's the matter?'

Finally he sat down. Not by her—on the same couch as her, but at the far end. 'I'm not sure what I'm doing here with you,' he said. 'We haven't always got on, have we?'

'We seem to have got on pretty well today. And after a doubtful start, we work well together. Come on, Gray. Tell me what's worrying you.'

'I had no business bringing you here. I wanted your company... I wanted it...very much indeed. But in four months I'm going back to Australia. You know that.'

'Of course I know it. And, since there's no way I'm going to lie to you, I'll tell you that I'll be very sorry indeed. But I'm a big girl and I make my own decisions.' She drank from her glass and held it out to him. 'Now pour me more wine and come and sit by me.'

She had to laugh at his bemused expression. 'No, I am *not* drunk,' she said. 'I'm quite aware of what I am doing.'

He seemed to come to a decision. First he filled her glass, then he came to sit by her—close this time. He took her hand, and she slid down so her head was on his shoulder. She felt so comfortable. The room, of course, was centrally heated, but from the partly open French windows in front of them came a touch of sea damp, and perhaps the distant smell of salt.

It was so comfortable there. His arm was round her now; she felt safe in his embrace. She thought she could hear the faint, faraway crash and hiss of waves; perhaps it was her imagination. He kissed her. At first he was tentative, his warm lips moving over her face, touching the high points of her cheeks, the side of her eyes, the softness of her neck. It was so good. But she knew that he was holding back, that there was something that still restrained him.

It was a time for decision, and she didn't hesitate. Putting her arms more firmly round him, she pulled him to her. This was something they would do together. But she was still a little fearful. His kiss was now harder, more demanding. She sighed, feeling her body become pliable, giving even. She knew she wanted him. But again he drew back.

His breathing was heavy. Even in that dim light she could see the passion in his eyes. 'Lucy, I'm not…we shouldn't…'

She knew what he was saying and loved him for it, giving her the last chance to draw back. 'What d'you mean, we shouldn't?' she asked. 'Of course we should. Now, come and kiss me again.'

He stood, reached down for her and pulled her to him, kissed her. Upright now, not cramped on the couch, their bodies could touch each other more fully. She was aware of her body and his as she opened her mouth under the pressure of his kiss. She could feel his hardness. Somehow she knew her own body's excitement, felt a similar hardening in the tips of her breasts. She had never felt anything like this with any man!

She did not know, perhaps for five minutes, perhaps for an eternity she stood there. Then she felt hands at the back of her dress, slowly, excitingly, feeling for the fastener. He slid his hand downwards. There was no sound but the tiny buzz of the zip, the distant roar of the sea, their own uneven breathing. His hands were now on her shoulders, and he eased her dress aside so that it fell in a silken heap round her ankles. The dark blue slip went with it. She kicked off her shoes, stood naked in front of him but for the scraps of white silk.

He stood back at arm's length, only his fingertips

touching the side of her. 'Lucy,' he groaned, 'you're so beautiful.'

Then he bent, lifted her effortlessly, laid her on the bed. As a gesture of acceptance, submission even, she lifted her arms over her head. 'You're wearing too many clothes,' she said.

She was a doctor, the sight of a man naked was not new to her, but still as he stripped she marvelled at his beauty. He had a lean athlete's body. And, unconcealed, there was the sign of his undeniable need for her.

He lay on the bed by her, kissed her again; she gave herself to the tumult of feelings, sensations. There was the ever-present murmur of the sea, the sound of traffic outside, somehow distant and unthreatening, even dim noises from the ballroom below. She could smell his cologne, and the distant but musky scent of his maleness. And when he kissed her she opened her mouth, he tasted so good.

She watched him with half-closed eyes, a dim body moving next to her own. Now there was more of her for him to kiss. She gasped with excitement as his mouth, his tongue, found places that gave her exquisite pleasure. Her bra was discarded, and she felt her breasts grow heavy with delight under his teasing caresses.

She had been passive for too long! She put her arms round his neck, pulled him down by her side so she could kiss him in her turn. Now her lips were roaming his body, feeling his excitement grow too. It was as good to give pleasure as to receive it.

But he couldn't remain passive for too long. She found herself recumbent again, her briefs somehow eased off. A last kiss, more daring than any before, that made her catch her breath and pant with ecstasy.

He was poised above her. She held him, crying softly, urging him on. There was the tiniest moment of discomfort, then she was with him and part of him. There was a rhythm that felt so natural and familiar, and yet was entirely new. It was so good! He became more urgent, she responded to his mounting excitement as her passion rose too, and then, with a joint cry torn from both of them, they reached the climax of their love. 'My darling,' he sobbed, but there was nothing she could say.

He lay on his front by her, his hand gently stroking her heated body. 'You're so good to me,' he whispered.

'You're good to me too,' she whispered back.

CHAPTER SEVEN

GRAY slept with Lucy, and they woke in the middle of the night to make love again. This time they were more relaxed, and it took longer, was in some way easier. Then they slept once more.

She was first awake in the morning. She felt strangely clear-headed. He lay by her side, hair tousled, the stern lines of his face erased by sleep. Somehow he looked more vulnerable. Perhaps she could catch a glimpse of the boy he might have been before he'd started the long fight to become a doctor and an athlete. She had an image of a different Gray, of a man who didn't hide behind his work and his dedication.

How did she feel? she asked herself. Basically she felt happy. She was content with what she had done. Any effect it would have on her future life was as yet uncertain, but she knew this was something that she would never regret. On the bedside table she saw discarded scraps of paper. Good, she had not wanted to ask him, not wanted to ruin the feeling of the time. But he had been careful; she would not get pregnant. He was a considerate man.

This man had moved her more deeply than anyone else in her life so far. What happened next between them was a matter for time to tell.

Slipping carefully out of bed, she pulled on her silk peignoir, padded over to the tray on the table and made two cups of coffee. She put one at each side of the bed, thought a minute, and then took off the peignoir before climbing back in. She had been naked all night; she would stay that way.

He woke, quickly; she saw doubt in the still-sleepy eyes. Kissing him on the forehead, she said, 'There's no hurry, no hurry. We're on holiday. There's a coffee waiting for you when you want it.'

Now his eyes flashed with awareness, with intelligence. 'Lucy, we...'

She kissed him again quickly. 'Never mind we, don't talk, don't worry about anything. When you're ready, sit up and drink your coffee.'

So he sat up, reached for the cup. When he held it, he asked, 'Lucy, why do I feel at a disadvantage? In this situation it's supposed to be the man who gets up first, who makes the decisions, says what needs to be said.'

'You're not at a disadvantage, and there's no situation. There's only you and me.'

'But last night we...'

'Last night was one of the best nights of my life,' she told him seriously. 'I shall never forget it. I have no, *no* regrets. But I don't want to hear any more about it, it'll only spoil things. I don't want an inquest. The future can take care of itself. For the moment you are going back to Australia and I am finishing my training.'

'You seem to have everything worked out.'

She couldn't tell whether he was happy with this, or uncertain. But she went on, 'There was an old Latin tag we learned at school—*carpe diem*. It means seize the day.' She giggled. 'But I don't think Miss Frith had quite this situation in mind when she told

us to adopt it as a motto. Seize the day. Make the
best of what you have while you have it.'

She still couldn't talk him out of his serious mood.

'Lucy, I know you were a virgin. Last night must
have meant something to you, we have to think about
it.'

'I was a virgin, yes, but there's no man I would
rather have given it to than you. I did so freely, happily. Now, shouldn't we be thinking about breakfast
and then getting on that plane?'

She saw him sigh. He knew she was going to have
her own way.

The rain of the night had cleared; yesterday's bracing
good weather had come back. They walked along the
front for a while, watching the waves crash onto the
rocks below. She was happy to be with him, holding
his hand, feeling his arm on her shoulders as he urged
her across the road. Then they went back to the hotel
and packed. Time to be in the air again.

Once they were flying, he tried to talk to her again.
'Lucy, I feel there are things we ought to get sorted
out. Last night…'

She kissed him on the side of the face again. 'I'm
still having the most marvellous weekend. I don't
want to talk, but if you insist we will. In a week.
When we've both had time to think. Until then I'm
still the humble SHO and you're the specialist registrar; nothing has changed between us.'

'Things certainly have changed,' he said heavily,
'and you know it as well as I do.'

Of course, she did know it. She just couldn't maintain the pretence to herself that things would be as

they were before. But for now she didn't want to think, to plan, to wonder. She was happy just to be.

It wasn't long before they were back on the ground driving back to Lizzie's in the centre of London. 'Do you feel a sense of anticlimax?' he asked as they drew up outside the flatlets.

'Of course I do. This weekend I will never forget, but it's hard to get back to the everyday world.' She thought a minute. 'I know we've both got things to do, but come up to my room a minute and we'll have a quick drink.'

She picked up her mail as they walked upstairs together, then left him in her room to make coffee. Then they sat side by side on her bed, a quick companionable kiss and she ripped open her letters. 'Anything interesting?' he asked.

'A letter from Francis Ponder. He wants me to go to dinner, on Friday night.'

'I've got that off too. I was hoping that we could...'

'I'm sorry,' she said gently, 'but I promised I'd help Francis with this. It's not a social meeting. He's hosting a party of people who might make a contribution to the hospital charity. He says the party will be impressed by the presence of what he calls a real Lady, especially as I am a doctor as well. I think I've got to go.'

'Why should you? You work hard enough as it is.'

'Possibly. But Francis makes sense, sober, he's quite efficient. You might not like what I am doing, but it will result in the hospitals getting funds, you can't deny that.'

'I know. I just don't like hospitals having to rely on...well, people like you having to put yourself out.'

Gently she put her arm round his neck. 'Don't

worry, Gray. And remember, you did your bit falling into the green gunge. It's just the same sort of thing.' She hesitated. 'D'you object to charity...because you were brought up in an orphanage?'

He looked at her darkly. 'You're too bright some-times, Lucy. You make me think about things I don't want to go into. Perhaps, yes, that's why I do object to...some charitable organisations. The orphanage did rely on charity to a certain extent. I was brought up, really well, by caring, kind people. But on occa-sions—just one or two—people who had contributed came around to visit. I suppose they were entitled to see how their money was spent. But I felt just a touch...observed.'

She thought about this; it troubled her. 'So my up-bringing must irritate you?'

'Not at all. I very much like your father, your brothers. Your upbringing doesn't irritate me. I envy it.'

She was carefully examining one of the younger chil-dren for signs of bruising when she was surprised to see Gray peer round the door of the ward. Didn't he have a clinic in another part of the building? 'What are you doing here?' she asked.

He put his arm round her shoulders, guided her behind a set of screens round a bed, now empty. 'Just heard,' he said, 'I've got to go back to Lally's hos-pital. There's been another emergency and they need a paediatric oncologist urgently again. The lady on-cologist there is trying to manage her job and her soon-to-come baby, and she's got elevated blood pressure and IUGR—intrauterine growth retardation. The baby's a bit small. I'm going to be there at least a week—I'll not be able to drop in to your room for frequent cups of cocoa.'

No one could see them, and he leaned forward and hugged her to him, kissed her. For a moment she gave way to him, then pushed him off and said mock seriously, 'Dr Woods! Remember my reputation. Wards are for work and…and…rooms are for…so I'll not see you for a while?'

'Afraid not. But can I phone you tonight? We'll see if we can sort something out.'

'I'd like that, I'll be in my room.' From the other side of the curtain came the sound of children's raised voices. 'Look, I'd better go. Phone me tonight.'

It was late when he phoned, and she sat on her bed in her dressing gown, listening to that attractive Australian burr. 'I know you said wait a week,' he said, 'but I didn't know that I'd have to move away from you. I've got a feeling of unfinished business, and I don't like it. Our weekend away was glorious— but we can't just ignore it.'

She might have guessed that he would feel this way. He wouldn't put off anything that he felt needed seeing to at once. 'Gray, I do still need time,' she said doubtfully. 'I've got to get things straight in my mind.'

'So do I. Look, things here are really hectic and I doubt I'll be able to get away before the middle of next week. But I've got to see you before then.'

'You can phone me at night,' she said, 'and I'm working on Saturday but I should get the evening off—how about if I come up to your hospital then?'

'Sounds good. You can't come to my room, it makes a Victorian workhouse look hospitable. But I'll find a local pub where we can have a chat. How are things on the ward?'

'We're missing you but we're coping,' she said airily. 'We had a new admission today…'

When she rang off she realised she was rather dreading having to talk seriously to Gray. She liked his company a lot, admired him. But she now recognised that over the past twelve years she had built up an armour that insulated her against too many romantic feelings. She was going to have to think seriously about what she felt about Gray.

Dinner with Francis was a success. She knew she was good at what she did. The group she was meeting was pleasant; they were impressed by her title and the fact that she was a working doctor. She gave a little talk about her work as a doctor and the work of the charity. Afterwards, she knew there would be generous donations.

'As usual, you did well,' Francis said as they had a non-alcoholic drink together afterwards. 'If you worked for me we could make a fortune. People listen to you, do what you want them to.'

'I wish you'd listen to me,' she said irritably, 'and why did you tell him that we had an understanding? He thought we were half engaged or something.'

'I wish we were,' Francis said imperturbably. 'And you can't blame a man for trying. I like Gray Woods anyway, he's a good man.'

Gray phoned her through the week, and she arranged to meet him at his hospital gates. Throughout the day she was worried; she still did not know what she was to say to him. She didn't even know what she wanted from him.

And then, an hour before the end of her shift, there was a frightened call from a nurse and the rattle of running feet. A nine-year-old girl's heart had just stopped. Lucy hit the alarm for the cardiac arrest team, ran over herself to give the blow to the chest that might restart the heart. Then there was the arrival of the arrest team, the apparent chaos. But the girl's heart was beating again, she was stabilised and then moved down into Intensive Care.

Lucy asked Lisa to phone Gray on his mobile, saying she would be delayed. And so she was over two hours later than she had intended.

There was a light rain falling, and the lights at the front of the hospital shone on the coat of the man who stepped out of the shadows and waved her car into a vacant parking slot. Then, unhurried, he walked over and slid into her passenger seat.

'Sorry,' she gabbled, 'I was going to be here before, I really was, but there was this case we had and I...'

He leaned over to kiss her on the cheek. His face was wet; there was something oddly intimate about the coolness of his touch. 'It doesn't matter,' he said. 'I'm a doctor like you, I know how things are. Now, how long since you ate?'

She looked at him as if he were mad. 'How long since I ate? What kind of question is that?'

'It's a sensible one. Are you going to give me an answer?'

It was good to hear his voice again! But she forced herself to concentrate on what he had asked her. 'It's been hectic on the ward,' she said. 'I had some cereal this morning and I pinched a bit of chocolate off Lisa but…'

'I thought so—you're showing all the classic signs of someone who's been too busy to eat. There should be a tattoo on the forearm of every young doctor saying keep your blood sugar up. You can leave the car here; let's get you fed before we do anything else.'

Five minutes later she was sitting in a small back room in a nearby pub, facing a plate with a pie in its own dish in the middle of it. When she stuck her fork through the golden crust, the smell that arose made her realise just how hungry she was. 'I'm ravenous,' she said, as if making a discovery.

'The food here is good. Now you just eat while I have a beer, and then we'll talk.'

It was surprising just how much better she felt when she had finished. The anxiety she had felt at meeting Gray, the impossibility of making a decision, all now seemed less important. She sighed happily, and reached for the wine he had fetched her. 'We can talk now,' she said. 'I hadn't realised just how… stressed I was.'

He nodded soberly. 'Hard time on the ward?'

'Yes, we had this girl in and she…'

He reached over and touched her lips with his finger. The tiny caress shocked her, silenced her. 'It doesn't matter now, you've left the ward. When you leave, you must learn to put the work behind you. Every doctor must learn it. Now, have your drink, say nothing for a few minutes and then we'll be able to talk. Okay?'

She took a deep breath. 'Okay,' she said, 'but you start.'

'Last weekend,' he said. 'I have to admit that I half

hoped…or expected…that something like what happened, would happen. But I didn't know that you were…'

'A virgin,' she supplied cheerfully.

'Quite. But it wasn't exactly that that made me feel…well, the way I do about you now.'

'How do you feel about me now?'

'I'm not quite sure. I think we've shared something that was wonderful. I want it to have a future. But…I know I have to go back to Australia in a few months.' He frowned, and she could tell he was perplexed.

'As a declaration of undying devotion that leaves a lot to be desired,' she told him.

'I know, I'm sorry. I told you, I just can't make sense of things. There's my feelings for you, and the fact that I know what I have to do. I don't like having things left undecided.' He looked at her, brow deeply furrowed. 'Anyway, tell me how you feel. It'll help me.'

What did she feel? Carefully, she said, 'I've spent so long fending off men that it's become almost a habit. First when I was wandering, and then when I was a student, I got plenty of offers. I turned them all down. I had things to do. Gray, I just can't make any kind of decision. We'll have to let things stay as they are for a while. You know, in medicine, it's often best not to make a decision until you've thought about all the possible factors.'

His expression was bleak. 'And sometimes if you don't act promptly, you lose the patient.' He sighed. 'But I can't think what to do myself, so, okay, decision postponed. Now…'

His bleep sounded. He pulled it from his belt, looked at the number and winced.

'Don't tell me, it's an urgent call,' she said. 'Don't worry, Gray, I'll be in touch. Now off you go. I'll finish my drink and pick up my car.'

'But, Lucy, you need as much as I do to—'

'Off you go!' she said, making shooing movements with her hands. 'There's no way we can decide anything now.' She leaned over to kiss him on the cheek. How many of their kisses had been hurried, last minute? 'Things are fine, I'll be in touch.'

He went. She sighed herself, and decided just for once to treat herself to another glass of red wine.

'What are you doing over Christmas?' Gray asked.

She shrugged. 'Work has to go on, I guess I'll be here. Since I don't have children myself I'm happy to let those who do have take the holiday. I'll do a few extra shifts and then have a break sometime in the new year.'

'Same with me,' Gray said. 'It'll be good to be working just with you.'

'It will be good,' she agreed, with a sad smile.

They were working through the list of their patients, trying to decide which of them could be sent home for at least Christmas Day and Boxing Day. Both knew how lonely a child could get in hospital at this time, no matter what the staff did to provide a party atmosphere.

She thought Gray had something on his mind. Since he had come back to Lizzie's they had stuck to their agreement not to talk about their future, not to make any decisions. She had enjoyed his company, looked forward to the snatched times they had together. But, like a dark cloud on the horizon, the time of his return to Australia loomed closer and closer.

'Have you anything planned for the beginning of February?' Gray asked tentatively.

Her heart lurched. Was he going to ask her away, take her somewhere as he had done before? How she hoped so! 'My brother Michael has invited me to his chalet to go skiing,' she said, 'but I haven't said yes or no yet. You could come too if you liked. Why, what have you got in mind?'

'Nothing,' he said dismissively, 'forget it. You go skiing with your brother.'

Anger rose in her. 'Don't ever tell me to forget it, Gray,' she snapped. 'If nothing more, we're friends. You can ask me anything.'

He had the grace to look ashamed. 'Sorry,' he said, 'didn't mean it. It's just that I've been asked on a sort of holiday, but not the sort you're thinking of. I've been asked—invited—to give five days to a charity. It's linked to the orphanage I was brought up in in Australia. They're taking a set of kids who have been ill to recuperate in the Lake District. Fourteen, fifteen, sixteen-year-olds. They need a resident doctor—that's me.'

'Is there room for another doctor?'

He looked sheepish. 'Well, if they had a female doctor they wouldn't need to pay a nurse. But I don't know if you...'

'Don't say it! You think that because I do a lot of work for charity by going to parties and so on, I might not want to do some of the actual work!'

'No,' he said. 'I know what you put in. I just thought that you might need an actual holiday.'

'And you don't? I'd love to come, Gray, so organise it for me, will you? Now, Hettie Sommers here...'

*　　*　　*

They walked side by side towards a chalet, looking across a flat valley to the snow-capped mountains beyond. It had been the kind of fine winter day that only the Lake District could produce. She took a deep breath; the air was so different from London!

They were in the grounds of Lenton Hall, an old grey-stone building. The hall itself held classrooms, a dining room, recreation rooms and a small sick bay. In the grounds were the four chalets, each centrally heated, that held the thirty children who were recuperating here.

Earlier in the day they had seen all the children individually, checked through their medical records and seen to a couple of injections. Most of the children were reasonably fit. There were three children who were in remission from leukaemia; Lucy, of course, took a special interest in them. Now it was recreation time, and Lucy had noticed that one of the leukaemia patients, an attractive fifteen-year-old girl called Laura Bell, wasn't present.

'She said she didn't feel like games,' one of the other children had told Lucy, 'so she's sitting on her bunk.'

Not a good start to what was supposed to be a holiday. Lucy and Gray had walked across to make enquiries.

Both heard the sounds coming from the little room. Laura was sobbing, the heartbroken sobs of someone who was half woman, half child. Gray frowned. 'This might need a woman's special touch,' he muttered to her. 'I'll wait for you on the verandah. Call me if it's anything medical.'

Lucy thought back over the afternoon. Perhaps Laura had been just a bit too obviously enjoying herself, showing the confidence that often hides a fear. Lucy had watched her pull straight her sweater several times, to emphasise her youthful figure. And she had refused to remove the brightly coloured tam-o'-shanter that hid her bald head. The other two patients just didn't care.

'It's Lucy,' Lucy said, tapping on the door. 'Dr Brett. May I come in, Laura?'

'No!' came the vehement answer. 'I don't want to see anybody. I'm all right.' Lucy went in anyhow.

She had had a lot of practice dealing with emotionally troubled children; it could be one of the most daunting parts of her job. The younger children often had no clear understanding of the seriousness of their condition, they were ill and that was all. But the fourteen, fifteen and sixteen-year-olds were aware that they had a dangerous illness, that they could die. Some dealt with it by refusing to believe in the condition, some took it stoically, a few were terrified.

'Go away,' Laura shouted as Lucy entered, then turned her back and pulled the sheet over her head.

Lucy stood a moment irresolute, then took a glass from the little table and poured orange juice into it. Then she rinsed through a flannel on the side of the basin, and brought both back to Laura's bunkside.

'Sit up, Laura!' she said firmly. 'If you're ill I need to know; if you're not, then I'll help in some other way. Now, rub this flannel over your face and then have a drink. It'll make you feel better.'

The habit of obeying doctors was engrained in Laura. She sat up as she was told. Lucy noticed with sadness that her first act was to make sure that her tam-o'-shanter was on firmly. Then, as instructed, she rubbed her face, drank the juice.

It took some delicate probing before Lucy managed to find out what was wrong. She might have guessed, it was boyfriend trouble. She had noticed the boy in question, Terry White, another leukaemia patient from the same hospital as Laura. He was tall, attractive, with a thin gray down of hair which, Lucy realised, was now very fashionable. And he'd been sitting, smiling at another girl from another hospital.

'We've seen a lot of each other at Clevelands,' Laura said, naming the hospital in the Midlands she had come from. 'Because we're about the same age, we have to. I used to have a boyfriend, but when I got ill he…disappeared and I thought…cos Terry and I got on so well…that…'

'He's not actually said anything to you?' Lucy asked.

'No. Not yet. But I thought we were getting so that…and he does seem to like me a lot. It's just this new girl he's suddenly met. We don't meet a lot of new people, you know. And then there's…' She indicated her head.

'But you're not really, well, going out together?'

'No,' said Laura. 'Dr Brett, Lucy, will you talk to him? Tell him that I…ask him if he wants…I don't know!' She burst into tears again.

Lucy put her arm around the girl, pulled her close. 'Love can be hard,' she said. 'You think you'll never survive, but you do.' Her mouth twisted wryly. She should be listening to her own good advice!

'So you will talk to him?'

It was not a good idea, Lucy told the girl again and again. But eventually she agreed. Someone would mention something to Terry. Then it was a case of getting Laura out of her bunk, splashing cold water on her face, lending her a lipstick and sending her back to the main hall.

'Whatever happens, you've got to fight!' she told Laura.

'Just like fighting leukaemia,' Laura said bitterly, 'and look where it's got me.'

But she went. And there was a set to her lips that convinced Lucy that, somehow, she'd be all right.

'All fifteen-year-olds have this kind of problem,' Gray told her later. 'And the hothouse atmosphere of a hospital ward doesn't make things any better.'

'That's no consolation to Laura. Gray, I know it's wrong, but I said someone would have a word with Terry White. Will you do it?'

'Me, an expert on love?' He looked gloomy. 'Yes, I'll do it. But I don't think anything will come of it.'

'You thought I was making a sacrifice coming here,' she told him two days later, 'but I'm not. I've spent a lot of my life outdoors, and I love this. I love hospital work, of course, but this is different.'

They were walking behind a group of the children as they walked along by the side of a lake, the two minibuses that would pick them up visible in the distance. There were other volunteer helpers who organised the actual walking, but when they found out that Lucy and Gray were both experienced and willing, they insisted that both come along.

The aim of the holiday was to stretch, but not exhaust, the children. It was to get them used to not being ill. There was always a danger that frequent stops in hospital would encourage a child to think that he or she was an invalid, and would stay that way for life.

'I'm enjoying myself too,' he told her. 'The only problem is, I can't see as much of you as I would like to.'

'We spend most of each day together,' she replied mischievously.

'Don't be awkward, young Brett. You know very well what I mean.' The trouble was that the staff had to double up in bedrooms. Nobody minded, it was that kind of operation. Lucy was sleeping in the same room as the head of catering, and Gray with one of the outdoor leaders. So it meant they didn't spend much time alone together.

But they were enjoying themselves. At night they went with the group to the local pub. She had forgotten the careless camaraderie she had shared in when she'd been a medical student, and it was rather nice to be reminded of it. On occasion they stole a kiss, but never more than that. They had a tacit understanding that their problems would be shelved till they got back. This suited her.

'How come you ended up a doctor, Lucy?' one of the helpers asked one evening as they sat in a corner of the pub. 'My daughter's thinking about medicine as a career. I just don't know what to tell her.'

'I can tell you how I got started,' Lucy said, relaxed by the warmth of the room and tired after a day in the open air. 'I was in a logging camp in North-West America, and one of the men was brought in—he'd had a really nasty accident with a chain-saw. Well, the paramedic wasn't around so I...' She told them the well-remembered story: her own initial terror, the recognition that if she didn't do it nobody would, the instructions by radio, the growing excitement as she decided that she was doing some good.

So wrapped up in her story was she, that she didn't realise how fascinated her audience was. Then she looked up to see them all staring at her in silence. Gray was behind them, the tray of drinks he had just fetched unheeded in his hands.

'I did just what anyone would have done in those circumstances,' she mumbled, a little unnerved.

'I don't think so,' one of the leaders said.

'You've never told me that story before,' he said to her later when they were sitting side by side. 'And I'd say you've gone up in my estimation. But it's the kind of thing I'd expect you to do. I think you could deal with anything.'

'Not exactly anything,' she told him.

Next day there was trouble, and like all trouble it started quietly. The group had split in two for the day; Gray was with the stronger party and Lucy with the weaker ones. They were walking a mountain road, climbing steadily, heading for a pass to take them into the next valley where the minibus would be waiting. Around them were odd patches of snow; they were going to reach the snowline. Joe Scott the leader kept looking thoughtfully at the clouds gathering overhead, but decided to press on.

As usual Lucy was walking at the back, keeping an eye out for those moving too slowly, those showing signs of fatigue. And this time it was Laura Bell who seemed to have trouble keeping up.

'I'm all right,' Laura gasped when Lucy asked her how she felt. 'I've enjoyed it all so far. Just today I feel a bit…tired.' Lucy looked at her for a moment, then walked up to see Joe.

'Laura's having trouble,' she said. 'Any chance of us getting her down early?'

Joe pursed his lips, looked at his watch, glanced at the sky. He didn't need to look at the map; he knew this bit of the country too well. 'The others are moving well,' he said. 'It would disappoint them to turn back now.' He thought a minute and Lucy said nothing, she knew this had to be his decision.

Eventually, 'If you follow that track down,' he said, pointing to a well-marked path, 'in about two miles it hits the road. Half a mile up the road there's a pub, The Dragon. They'll let you shelter in the back, make you a cup of tea till the minibus calls. Will you take Laura down if I push on with the rest?'

It was a good decision. 'Happy to,' said Lucy.

'You've got your radio in case of trouble?'

'In my pocket. And my map, compass, first-aid kit, space blanket and even a length of safety rope.'

'Good,' said Joe, who took his responsibilities seriously. 'Off you go, then. Any trouble—call.'

Laura accepted being taken off the walk very readily—a sign that she was more tired than she had realised. But when they started moving downhill she picked up a little.

'I'm enjoying this no end,' she told Lucy. 'I think I'll join a rambling club when I get home.'

Then the bad weather hit them. At first there was just a vicious wind, sweeping round their collars, whipping at their legs. It didn't matter, both were well wrapped up. Then the rain started, cold and biting on their faces. Again, no problem, they were dressed for this kind of thing. But Lucy shivered, and thought she'd be glad to get onto the road.

For some time now a stream had followed the side

of the path, splashing and chattering. Now they had to cross it, on a bridge of two or three rough planks of wood. There was no hand rail. Obviously feeling better, Laura burst ahead, trotted over the bridge. The planks were greasy, wetted by the rain. Before Lucy could call out a warning Laura had slipped. There was time for one quick cry and then she fell into the pool beneath the bridge.

The water was near freezing. Lucy dashed to the bank, waded thigh deep into the fast-moving stream, helped Laura to her feet. Together they stumbled out and stood in the lee of a great rock, Laura coughing and spluttering. 'I'm cold,' she muttered through now-chattering teeth.

'Did you hurt yourself when you fell in?' Lucy demanded. 'Did you hit your head or anything like that?'

'N-no. I just fell on my back. Can we get going, Lucy? Perhaps I'll warm up then.'

But Lucy knew that if their wet clothes were subject to the full blast of the wind, they would never get warm. The wind-chill factor was high; Laura would quickly be subject to hypothermia. 'Wait here,' she said, and climbed to the top of the rock that was sheltering them. She had to report to Joe, the team leader. They were both still his responsibility. Thank God he had made her carry the small radio.

Joe's voice crackled. 'You're at the bridge over the stream? Can you see a small building about three hundred yards downstream?'

Lucy peered through the murk. Yes, there it was, a grey-stone huddle in a corner of a field. 'I can see it.'

'That's the Eastern Climbers' Association hut. I

know them well. Go to the front door, there's a key hidden in a crack just to the right of the bottom hinge. Inside you'll find food, blankets, a big oil stove. Get Laura warmed up and then call me back. Does she need medical assistance?'

'I am a doctor,' Lucy said frostily.

'Sorry. You can cope?'

'There's no need to worry if I can get her warm again in the next ten minutes.' Lucy shut off the radio and slithered back towards Laura.

The weather had now come down hard, the wind increased and the biting rain was turning to sleet. Lucy put her arm round Laura and urged her down towards the climbing hut. After the first two hundred yards she knew she had made the right decision. Laura's pace was slowing, her speech becoming slurred and she was getting irritable. All the classic signs of hypothermia.

They reached the hut. The key was hidden where Joe had said it would be. Rapidly Lucy looked round inside. It was like so many other huts she had visited. Laura slumped on a bench as Lucy started the oil stove; fortunately it was one of a kind she had dealt with before.

Soon the heat was radiating through the once-icy room. Lucy stood Laura in front of the stove, pulled off her sodden clothes and wrapped her in two blankets she took from the bunk room. Then she stretched two silver space blankets round her. After a moment's thought she took off her own boots, socks and trousers, and hung them over the rack to dry.

In a kitchen cabinet she found food stored; there was dried milk, cocoa and sugar so she made them both a drink. In a tin there were chocolate biscuits.

And when they had both eaten and drunk, she decided to examine her patient.

It was hard to tell without a thermometer, but she decided that Laura's external temperature was reasonable. Of course, her core temperature would be down, but if she was kept warm this would slowly return to normal. Laura was yawning now, the sleepiness just the kind of reaction Lucy had anticipated. She went outside and radioed Joe again.

'Never trust Lake District weather,' Joe said laconically. 'I never expected this storm. We had to come off early ourselves. How's Laura?'

'She's fine, sleepy now, but I think she's rather enjoying the adventure. Joe, it might be an idea to stay here in the hut if we can. I don't fancy moving her again if it's not necessary.'

'Going to suggest that myself. I'll phone and square it with the club committee. If you're sure you're all right we'll pick you up tomorrow morning. Is there enough food?'

'Simple stuff, but we'll not starve. Tomorrow morning, then?'

'Any problem, radio me. Otherwise, some time after nine.' Joe signed off.

Lucy decided to make Laura a larger meal before putting her to bed in one of the adjoining bunk rooms—after all, it was still quite early. She opened a tin of stewing steak and made some instant potato— not exactly a gourmet meal, but Laura appeared to enjoy it.

'You've been good to me, you and Dr Woods,' she said. 'I like my own doctors, but I wish you and him were with me in Clevelands. I've really enjoyed this stay.'

Delicately, Lucy asked, 'You got things sorted out with Terry White?'

'Oh, yes. He said Dr Woods had a word with him, explained that I was a bit…confused about things. So me and Terry had a good talk. He said that, with being in hospital so much, he didn't get chance to meet other girls. It was just a bit of…well, I can understand that. So we're still friends and we'll see how things go when we get back. Are you in love, Lucy?'

The question was so unexpected that Lucy didn't know what to answer. 'Well…I don't know,' she said. 'There's a man in my life but…I'm training to be a doctor and there isn't much time…so we sort of don't think about it.'

'You should try having cancer,' Laura said calmly. 'If nothing else it teaches you how valuable time is.' She yawned again. 'Shall I go to bed now?'

Lucy had made them both beds up in one of the bunk rooms, fortunately one with a background heater. Laura was soon asleep, and Lucy wandered round the hut, tidying as best she could, and slipping on her now dry trousers. Then she settled to try to read one of the tattered paperbacks that had been left. She couldn't concentrate. Laura's question about being in love had bothered her. And her further comment about how valuable time was had bothered her further.

Outside the storm roared with undiminished fury. Lucy put down her book, and stared with unseeing eyes at the red-glowing oil stove. Then lights flashed across the windows of the hut, and she heard the harsh rattle of a diesel engine. Who could that possibly be? Warily, she went to the front door. There was a knock. 'Lucy!' called a voice. She recognised the voice. It was Gray.

'I'd finished all the medical duties,' he said, taking packages out of a cardboard box he had brought in, 'and Joe said there wasn't much chance of us doing very much tomorrow morning. And he said he'd feel happier if there were two of us up here with Laura. So I borrowed a Land Rover, bought a few things and came up to see you. I thought we might have a picnic. And tomorrow morning we'll bump back down the track taking Laura with us.'

They had both been in to see the sleeping girl, and decided that she had come to no great harm. And Lucy discovered that she was suddenly hungry. She hadn't fancied the meal she had managed to cook for Laura, but now she was ravenous.

She might have guessed that Gray could cook. He poured her a glass of the oaky red wine that they both liked and then moved into the kitchen. It was a simple meal but a good one: first a grilled steak with a pre-mixed salad and warmed bread rolls and then sweet pancakes, which he flambéed in brandy. Afterwards they sat side by side, glass of wine in hand, gazing at the stove.

He put his arm round her, kissed her. 'Getting late,' he said. 'Where am I to sleep? I've brought a sleeping bag.'

'Well, Laura and I are in what I think is the girls' bunk room. There's a heater in it. This room is warm now, why don't you sleep in here? You could fetch a mattress and put it in front of the stove.'

'Good idea. Incidentally, I raided your room.

There's a bag of things that I thought you might need overnight. Toothpaste and so on.'

'That was thoughtful of you.' She took the offered carrier, peered in it and blushed slightly. 'I see you've brought me a change of underwear.'

'I thought you might have got wet. Want to help me with the mattress?'

They went into the men's bunk room and dragged a mattress back into the living room. Lucy went to peer at Laura. 'Fast asleep,' she reported, 'and she's not going to wake.'

It was when they were kneeling facing each other, on each side of the mattress. He rolled open his sleeping bag and then unzipped it. She rubbed her hand across the dark blue lining. 'It feels warm,' she said. 'Comfortable.'

His voice was husky. 'There's room for two. If they get very close.'

He said nothing more. The silence between them grew—and then she decided. She walked over to the door; just as a precaution she locked it. Then she switched off the light and the room was bathed in a red glow from the stove.

He came to her, took her by the hand and led her towards the mattress. While they were still standing he pulled the sweater over her head, unbuttoned her plaid shirt and took off that too. There was only her bra left. He reached round her and then that too slipped to the floor.

'You too,' she muttered. In his turn he waited as she stripped off his shirt and sweater. The red glow turned his face and body into a pattern of light and shade. She ran her fingers across the muscles of his arms and chest, looked up to see his face, intent, absorbed.

'You're lovely,' he said.

He didn't take her in his arms then, but seemed content, as she was, to run the tips of his fingers over her body. She sighed as he cupped her, felt her breasts grow heavy with anticipation. She touched him too, guessed at the darkening of his eyes as she rubbed through the fine maze of hair on his chest.

He reached for the clasp of her belt, undid it, then eased down all the clothes she had left. She was naked. He led her to the mattress, gently laid her on it. There was the rustle of his own clothes, and then he was by her side. He reached to her, gathered her to him.

Their love-making was gentler than before; both had had a long day. But still she knew he was caring for her, carrying her with him so that together they reached a climax that was ecstatic and so, so comfortable. Then for a while she lay in the crook of his arm, and slept. But not too long.

'I must go,' she whispered to him. 'I don't want Laura to wake and find me not there.'

'If you must,' he whispered back, and she knew he understood. He said, 'Lucy, you make me so happy.'

'You make me happy too.' She grabbed her clothes and scampered out of the room.

For a few moments next morning she wondered where she was when she woke. Her eyes travelled over the rough walls, the beams of the ceiling. There was the patter of rain against the window and then she smelled coffee. Gray must be already up.

Life seemed so good to her. She thought of the

night before, a smile on her lips. Gray made her so happy, he…

It struck her, with the force of the wind that slammed against the walls of the climbing hut. There was no doubt about her feelings now, they were certain, as fixed as the rocks in the fields around her. She was in love.

The certainty left her feeling bewildered. She loved Gray Woods. The question was, did he love her? And what was she going to do now?

There was always something vaguely depressing about the end of a holiday. Not that it had been a holiday really, and not that she wasn't looking forward to being back at work at Lizzie's. But she felt a bit—desolate.

They were driving down from the Lake District, cruising slowly through the industrial landscape of Birmingham. She had offered to drive Gray in her Vitara—it had seemed the easiest way to get them both up to and back from the camp. Now he was sitting casually by her side, and every now and then she glanced at him. He looked gorgeous!

Gray had driven her and Laura back to the camp the next morning. They'd given Laura a thorough examination; there were no ill effects. And the next day was the end of their stay. Lucy had said, sincerely, how much she had enjoyed herself, and promised to come again, if she could get away from hospital. Gray had pointed out that he would be back in Australia in two months.

'When I see this landscape, I want to go back to the Lake District,' he told her. 'Who could live in this smoke when there's clear air up there?'

'Lots of people have to live here,' she snapped. 'There's just no choice.'

He looked at her, obviously a little surprised at the sharpness of her tone. 'I know that,' he said, trying to calm her. 'It's just that I had such a good time up there. It was so pleasant to spend so much time with you, Lucy. You know you've got to be something really special to me.'

'So you tell me.' Her voice was still abrupt. 'But you're still going back to Australia in a couple of months.'

'Yes,' he said flatly. 'I'm going back to Australia.'

'So we'd better get used to the idea of not seeing each other, hadn't we?'

The rest of the journey took place in silence.

CHAPTER EIGHT

TECHNICALLY, it was nurses' work. But Lucy had never believed that there was a clear demarcation between doctor and nurse, and was always willing to help when she could.

Eight-year-old Jenny Chapman had the rarer acute myeloblastic leukaemia. Her treatment had left her very susceptible to infection, and she was now in reverse barrier nursing—all visitors had to wear sterile caps, gown and masks. This was difficult for Jenny's parents, and frightening for the child herself. After checking her thoroughly, Lucy sat by the bed and tried to teach the little girl relaxation techniques.

'Squeeze your toes tightly together,' she whispered, 'then squeeze your legs and thighs really hard. Now wait a minute, then relax them. Just let your legs wobble. Just pretend that if you leave them they might float up to the ceiling.'

Dutifully, Jenny did as she was told. After half an hour Lucy thought that she might have got somewhere. It was difficult teaching a child in pain to relax. But if it could be done, the child would benefit.

After the excitement of the stay in the Lake District Lucy found it hard to relax herself. It was even harder because she now knew that she loved Gray. Before, the central fact of her life, her main concern, had been her work. Now work came second. She thought of Gray first thing in the morning when she woke, last thing at night before she slept, in every possible minute in the day when she didn't have to concentrate on something else. She had never dreamed love could be like this!

It amazed her, looking back, that she had not known it before. Her love had grown almost unnoticed as she had worked with him, come to know him better. Then it had burst on her, like one of the titanic storms she had marvelled at in the American North-West. She loved Gray Woods. It was the central fact of her existence.

Did he love her? Certainly he had never said so. She was inexperienced, she didn't know what to expect, but during their love-making she would have expected him to say something. He hadn't. Of course, in many ways she knew he was a reticent man, not accustomed to showing his emotions. But surely he could have given her something?

One thing was certain. She had her pride. He was the man; she was the woman. She would not say anything to him, not hint, not suggest, not ask, not beg. If he wanted to go back to Australia, then there was no way she would try to stop him. She was tough, resilient, she could take it.

But you've never felt like this before, a tiny voice told her. It's not going to get better.

He hadn't phoned her, called round to her room. After the conversation of the motorway, she hadn't really expected him to. As she had said, they would have to get used to the idea of not seeing each other.

As was usual after a holiday, there was a fair amount of catching up to do. Children who had been sent home for Christmas with their families were back in, the day clinics were fuller than ever. She caught glimpses of Gray every now and again, but they seldom had time for anything but a quick exchange of smiles. I wonder what he's thinking, she asked herself. She didn't ask him.

It was four days after she had started work again. She had just worked solidly for twelve hours, she was sitting on the bed in her room, trying to work up the strength to get undressed and have a shower. Then all she wanted was sleep.

Her phone rang. She looked at it malevolently. If it was the ward she was *not*, she was just *not* going back. There were limits. But it wasn't the ward, it was her father. She smiled to herself; it was good to talk to him.

'I know how busy you are,' he said after they had gossiped about friends and family, 'but could you get away Sunday night? I've got a surprise for you, rather a pleasant one, I think. Come to dinner.'

'One of your special dinners?' she asked cautiously. 'The bright and the great and the famous? I don't think I'm up to it at the moment.'

'Nothing like that. Just a few friends. In fact, see if you can bring Gray along, if he can get away. Your brothers are always asking about him. We'll have a pleasant relaxed time.'

'I can only ask him, though he's busy too. But I'm sure I can get away.'

It gave her a bitter-sweet thrill to think of Gray in the company of her family. They all liked him. Of course, they had no idea of her feelings for him. She was very fond of her family, but she had been a loner for too long to be able to confide in any one of them.

Next morning she managed to catch Gray as he made a flying visit to the ward. He looked tired, dis-

tracted. But when she told him of the invitation, he
accepted at once.

'I can take the time off, I'm entitled to it. And I
really like your family, Lucy. They make me wish I
had one.'

They could be your family too, a voice in her head
clamoured, but all she did was smile and say, 'Families can be mixed blessings.'

He waved his arm at the noisy ward behind him.
There were a dozen parents sitting by their children,
reading, talking, playing games. 'Parents make our
job easier,' he said, 'even if they are a pain at times.'

'True.' She didn't want this kind of conversation,
not now, not here. She wanted him to herself. 'Shall
I drive you there next Sunday?'

He shook his head. 'I'd like it, but I don't know
when I'll be able to get away. I'll take a taxi.'

Well, at least she'd be seeing him out of the hospital. That was something.

It was a small family gathering and she was enjoying
it. They sat in her father's small panelled drawing
room, sipping sherry and making small talk. At one
end of the room she could see her father and her
brother Michael listening to Gray. Her father and
brother had that intent look that she knew so well—
whatever Gray was telling them, it merited serious
thought. A quick pain lanced through her. Gray got
on so well with her family. They would welcome him
as one of them. But...

She was sitting on the couch where her brother
James had pulled her so they could have a private
talk. His wife Marion hadn't felt up to dinner—she

was now nearer to having their first baby. And James, the imperturbable financial genius, was near to panic.

'She is an older mother, Lucy,' he said. 'I know we've got the best people helping her—but I still worry.'

'James, there's no need. She's going to be all right. Having a baby isn't being ill, it's a perfectly normal, natural process, like eating or sleeping. She'll be fine. And she's not an older mother—not these days.'

'She doesn't feel fine. She says she feels awkward, uncomfortable, can't even get out of a chair without help. She can't wait to get it over with.'

For a moment Lucy thought about telling him that some babies grew so large that they temporarily displaced the mother's heart, and then decided it wasn't a good idea. 'Just you wait. She'll have the one, he or she will be beautiful and then you'll both be thinking about a second.'

She saw her father leave the room; apparently his guest had arrived. She knew someone else was invited but she didn't know who. Turning back to James, she said, 'I'll pop round to see Marion next week some time. That's if she's not fed up with doctors. By now she must...'

Behind her, her father re-entered the room. She heard him say, 'I'll introduce you to my family, but of course you already know...'

An American voice said, 'I already know Dr Lucy Brett. Lucy, I knew you'd do it. I said I'd come to get you when you qualified, and I have.'

She turned, amazed. She hadn't seen him in over six years, but he hadn't changed. The same stocky, muscular body, the happy smile, the impression of instant energy. She stood, and was instantly hugged, kissed, lifted off the floor. She saw Gray's surprised face looking at her. What was Royston Rogan doing here?

'I'm going to make my home in London now,' Royston explained when they were seated round the dinner table. 'I decided it was time to make a few changes. My wife died eighteen months ago, and after that I felt I didn't want to hang around Seattle much longer. So I decided to concentrate on the shipping and hand over the logging to young Harry. My brother sends his good wishes, by the way, says any time you're over there to call in. He says he thinks of you every time he takes his shirt off and sees the scars.' Royston laughed. 'That accident was dreadful, but it certainly cured him of taking chances. Now he's more safety conscious than I was, and that's saying something.'

'What accident was that?' James asked, and Royston told the table about how she had saved his brother's life, following instructions sent over the radio. To much laughter, he then told everyone about how he had taken her to dinner and she had been announced as Lady Lucy Brett, to the annoyance of Miss Tremblett.

Lucy sat at the dinner table, her head bowed. She liked Royston, he had been good to her, helped her, and she was grateful to him. But she wished desperately that he had not turned up now. Her life now was…difficult. From time to time she glanced at Gray, but his head was carefully turned away; he would not meet her eyes.

'I know you're busy,' Royston went on expansively, 'but if you could spare the odd hour here and there, I could do with your help. I'm looking for a house. I've got one or two in mind—perhaps you'd walk round them with me and tell me what you think. Sort of give me the woman's opinion.'

'I don't have much time, Roy, but I'd be happy to help if I can.' What else could she say?

It turned out that Royston knew people who knew her father. He had called, introduced himself, and the two men had instantly got on. Like her father and her two brothers, Royston was a money man. He talked their language. But most of the time he apparently wanted to talk to her.

As they were drinking coffee after dinner she managed to have a quick word with Gray. 'I knew Royston in America,' she told him. 'He helped me get started as a medic.'

'He obviously has a very high opinion of you,' Gray observed courteously.

She felt like screaming. She hated it when he spoke to her in his polite, distant manner. She had slept with him, given herself to him! Didn't that matter?

'His wife was very ill, in a coma,' she said. 'He used to take me to dinner, but that was all.'

'I'm sure it was.'

Still the pleasant but distant voice. That did it. She would excuse herself to no one; he must think what he liked.

Shortly afterwards the butler came in and said there had been a call from St Elizabeth's Hospital, could Dr Woods possibly go back there?

'But you're not on call,' Lucy protested. 'They can't fetch you back now.'

'They can if I'm needed,' Gray said, 'so I really must make my apologies and go.'

'Let me run you back?'

'There's absolutely no need, Lucy. I'll take a taxi. You stay here with your friends and family.' And he was gone.

'It's a hard life being a doctor,' Royston said.

For the rest of the evening she more or less enjoyed herself, talking over old times with Royston, chatting with her family. But she still left early, pleading the pressure of work the next day.

As soon as she was back in her room she phoned Gray. 'You set up that call back to hospital, didn't you?' she asked. 'There was no need for you to come back?'

She heard him sigh. 'I should have known that I couldn't deceive you. Yes, Lucy, I did set up the call. I've been sitting here in my room.'

'Why? I thought you enjoyed our company.'

'I very much do. But I thought I'd leave you to spend some time with your friend. He seems a pleasant chap, who obviously wants to spend time with you. And I'm going to Australia soon, he's staying here. He obviously wants to marry you or something.'

'And, of course, you *don't*!' She slammed down the phone. She was glad to see Roy. But why, oh, why did he have to come now?

'Exciting times,' Sister Lisa Fletcher said to her on the ward next morning. 'Men come and men go. We're losing our lovely Dr Gray Woods.'

'Losing him? How are we losing him?' Lucy hoped Lisa didn't detect the panic in her voice.

'He's gone for three weeks to some hospital in the Midlands. Something about him getting the broadest possible experience while he is here.' Lisa sniffed.

'He'll not get better experience than he will at Lizzie's.'

'But how…when…who arranged it?'

'Apparently he's always had the option. He arranged it late last night. The consultant says he thought he was happy here, but it's probably a good idea for him to work in another part of the country, if only for a while. Now, d'you want me to come with you to have a look at that new admission…?'

Lucy didn't know what to think. But she had a good idea that Gray had gone to get away from her. And she wanted to know why.

That evening she rang him on his mobile. 'Why did you go without saying goodbye?' she asked without preamble. 'You knew you were going last night.'

His voice was as remote as before. 'I will be back in a few weeks, Lucy,' he said. 'There was no need to say goodbye. But can you give my apologies to your father again?'

'So what are you doing up there?'

'Oh, there's a lot of work here, you'd find it interesting. I saw a Wilms' tumour this afternoon, stage four, and we're hoping to…'

Usually she would have been fascinated. But not this time. However, she let him tell her, and made the usual interested noises.

'So when will you see Royston again?' he asked suddenly.

She desperately wanted to explain to him that Royston was a good friend but nothing more. But Gray had angered her—she saw no reason why she should explain her life to him.

'He's going to phone me,' she said. 'We're going house-hunting together.' The minute she had said it, she knew it had been the wrong thing to say. But she couldn't unsay it.

'That'll be nice for you,' she heard his cool reply. 'You'll probably see a lot of him in future. Must sign off now, Lucy, my bleep's going, we're made busy here. See you some time.'

She thought it was the worst phone call of her life.

Going out with Roy gave her a sad satisfaction. He was an old friend, she liked him and took pleasure in his company. But not as much pleasure as she took in Gray's company. They looked round three houses and eventually decided on one high on Hampstead Heath. 'I need to be able to see some distance,' he told her. 'I want a better view than the front of my neighbour's house.'

The next step was furniture. As ever, Roy was moving with American speed. He'd decided on the house, now he needed something inside it. She just didn't have the time to help; instead she would introduce him to Francis Ponder.

'Francis has a vast number of contacts and very good taste,' she told him. 'He's quite well off, but not as rich as you. You can pay him a commission if you like. But make sure he's sober when he's working for you.'

'You know my views on drinking when you should be working.'

Francis got to know them pretty quickly too. Lucy had to hide a grin when she overheard Royston 'interviewing' Francis. 'I pay well and I get good results. Good results means no drinking—if I so much as see you chewing a wine gum while you're on my time, then that minute you are out. Understand?'

'I am sure we will work well together,' Francis said, his voice just a little shaken. He'd never met anyone quite like Royston before.

And ten days later Royston invited her to dinner. 'Not a milk and sandwich supper, but a real proper meal,' he told her over the phone. 'Say seven-thirty. I can't pick you up cos I'm busy with meetings and so on till late, but I'll send a car round for you. You're not to drive or take a taxi—what's the use of money if you don't spread it around a little?'

'All right,' she said. 'I fancy a meal out.' She didn't say it might cheer me up, but she felt it.

Because she was miserable, she felt she had to make an effort, and went to some trouble to dress smartly. The hire car picked her up and took her to Martin's, a restaurant that she knew to be very expensive, and making itself a reputation. Typical of Royston to have found out about the place.

The *maître d'hôtel* greeted her as if she was an honoured guest, showed her to a booth and explained that Mr Rogan had phoned, he apologised but would be just a few minutes late. Would she like a drink? A glass of champagne, perhaps?

Lucy hid a smile. Royston had obviously been spreading his money here too. He once had told her in Seattle that he always got good service because he paid for it.

Ten minutes later he arrived. He bent over to kiss her, and then stood, arms wide, with a big smile. 'What d'you think of the suit?'

She recognised the cut at once. 'Don't tell me, you're going native. That's a Saville Row suit, I'm sure.'

'Too right it is. Bit more figure fitting than the American article but I like it. Let's order.'

He ordered with typical speed and then pushed aside the menu and said, 'I'm not here for the food, I've come to talk to you. I love London, I love the people, I'm going to stay. And what once might have been true isn't true any more. Your businessmen are *good*!'

'I'm glad you're happy.' She began to eat the fan of melon on raspberry coulis that she had picked as a first course. 'How's the furniture hunting going?'

'Going well. Francis now understands that I can make up my mind quickly. The house purchase is going through too—I can see myself moving in inside a month.'

She blinked. But then, Royston had always been able to get things moving. 'Everything's going well for you, then,' she said lightly.

'Nearly everything. When Amy died…well, as you know, she'd been in a coma for years. But it was still a shock, and I was surprised at how long it took me to get over it. Now, change of subject. How long since you took a holiday?'

She looked at him uncertainly. 'That's an odd question. You're the man who never took holidays, you would rather work. In fact I had a few days up in the Lake District a couple of weeks ago.'

'I heard about it. You were helping at a kids' camp, that was work. How long before you can have—say, two whole weeks to yourself?'

She was still unsure why he was asking. But she answered, 'In about six weeks I'll finish this tour of duty. I should have a fortnight off then.'

'Good. I'm thinking of hiring a yacht to tour a bit

of the Mediterranean. Get myself some culture, see Greece and so on. I want to have a proper party—a few friends from the States will come over. Would you like to come, Lucy? Come as a friend, I mean, no funny stuff, have your own room and so on. I'd really like you to.'

She had a definite image of Royston Rogan. He was a tough man, a shrewd businessman, hard-working, ruthless if necessary. He was capable of friendliness, generosity too. But as she looked into his eyes she saw another side to him. Royston Rogan was lonely. And, although she was tempted, that meant that there was only one possible answer she could give him.

'Roy, I'd love to, but I can't. I think I know what you're offering, even if you don't. I like you tremen-dously, you did a lot for me, you had faith in me when I didn't have much in myself. So I'll be brutally frank. I value your friendship. But we'll never be more than friends.'

For a while he was silent, his head bowed. Then he looked up and smiled. 'You remind me of a couple of Limey businessmen I've met. You don't believe in wrapping things up so there's any doubt. And I guess I like it. Okay, offer withdrawn. Now…tell me, it's that fellow Gray, isn't it?'

How could he know that? Not even her father, her brothers had spotted it. She stared at him, perplexed.

'Come on, I'm your friend,' he said. 'There are times you need to confide in someone, and I guess this is one of them. What's the problem?'

'How d'you know there's a problem?'

'I saw the way he was looking at you at your dad's

party. He thought no one else could see him, but I did. Now confess to Uncle Royston.'

So she told him. 'I...think he loves me, but he's going back to Australia. He's only here on a short contract and it's up in a month or so.'

'Does he know you love him? Have you told him that?'

'Well, no, I...of course I haven't told him...I do love him but I don't do things like that.'

'British reserve as usual,' he said. 'Are you sure you won't change your mind and marry me?'

'It's the best offer I'm likely to get,' she said morosely, 'but, thank you, no.'

From his pocket he took a mobile phone and pushed it across the table to her. She looked at it, scandalised. 'You aren't allowed to phone from here!'

'I know, I left my spare at the door. But no one is looking. Now, you know his number, phone him now and tell him you love him. Then see what happens.'

She stared at the phone, small, black, and absolutely impossible to pick up. 'I can't,' she said sadly. 'It's just not me.'

He reached for the phone. 'In that case let me fill your glass. Now we'll just eat, drink and reminisce like old friends. Did I tell you how Harry was getting on with the logging...?'

She felt better when she got back to her little room. She'd enjoyed the meal and the company; Roy was an amusing, witty companion. But, underneath, she knew she was miserable. She was missing Gray, and she didn't know how she'd get used to it.

It was raining. It had been raining all day; it looked like it might rain all night. When Gray had first come to England, he'd found the odd shower of rain different and vaguely refreshing. But now he was fed up with it.

Reyes Midland Hospital was large; like Lizzie's it had a worldwide reputation. It had some wonderful buildings, laboratories, wards. It also had more than a few buildings from the turn of the century, constructed of gloomy grey stone. He sat in his room in one grey building, looking across the darkened car park at another grey building.

Gray felt gloomy himself. In front of him was an opened letter, from an old friend in Australia. There was a handful of photographs, taken at the party when he'd left. 'Life is good and life is fast,' his friend Mike had written. 'Why don't you come and join in?' Mike had just been made a consultant neuro-surgeon; once they had had lots of cases in common.

He looked at the photographs again—of beaches, barbecues, a couple of friends on a boat. Life there looked so good. His sense of humour hadn't entirely deserted him; he'd shown the pictures to a couple of the staff on the ward. Their envy had been obvious. 'You know we all hate you,' the sister had sniffed.

There was a job waiting for him in Australia—he had been promised it when he'd left. In another six weeks he was going back to Australia, six weeks after that he would probably be made consultant. Now he realised he wasn't looking forward to it. He wanted to stay in England. He looked out of the window again. Just the drumming of the drops against the window, the reflections of the lights on the wet concrete. The weather in England was terrible!

Three weeks ago he had been called in by his consultant, Adam Harrison, at Lizzie's. 'Just for a five-minute chat,' Adam had said. 'Would you like a sherry?'

The conversation that followed was amiable, almost casual. Adam said that he had enjoyed working with Gray, that he had contributed a lot. Was he sure he wanted to go back to Australia? Of course, he wouldn't dream of poaching good men from a sister hospital—but if Gray wanted a full-time job in Lizzie's, then something could probably be arranged. Gray loved the way they did business here.

But work wasn't the reason he wanted to stay. He wanted to be with Lucy. He thought back over the time he had known her. She could be irritating; she could be too independent. She had a mind of her own and she didn't hesitate to say what she felt. After the last time, he had sworn never to let a woman get between him and his work. He was dedicated to it. He knew that he could find female companionship that was pleasant, undemanding and that didn't interfere with his work. Why then was he so keen on Lucy?

Anyway, there was this fellow Royston Rogan. He had only seen him once, and had disliked him on principle. However, he had to admit that, although older than Lucy, he seemed a pleasant enough man, and would probably be a good husband... What was he thinking? But Lucy obviously knew Royston well, was fond of him and...

The phone rang. Surely not—he couldn't be called out again? He had been hard at it all day. It was the porter at the residency lodge.

'There's a gentleman to see you, Dr Woods. Says his name is Royston Rogan... Yes, sir, an American gentleman, I think.'

Gray just couldn't believe it. He had been thinking about the man that very minute—how could he call downstairs? Was he working too hard? Was he suffering from delusions?

'Did you say Royston Rogan?' he asked again.

'Yes sir,' the porter answered, and added again, as if it explained a lot, 'an American gentleman.'

'Tell him I'm coming down,' he said.

It was the man he had met before at Lucy's father's house. He was dressed in an expensive blue suit, had a quiet smile. Though he was not Gray's favourite man in the whole world, there was no reason not to accept the outstretched hand.

'You're surprised to see me,' Rogan said. 'I don't blame you, I'm surprised to be here myself. There's a pub just across the road, why don't we go and have a drink? You're not still on duty, are you?'

'We do have some time off,' Gray said, 'so I'll come for a drink. What can I do for you, Mr Rogan?'

'Call me Royston—or Roy, I prefer. And it's more a question of what I can do for you...'

CHAPTER NINE

Lucy thought she was losing her enthusiasm. A lot of the SHO's work was very tedious, but vitally necessary. She had used to recognise this, and still enjoy doing it. But now it was losing its excitement.

This morning as she walked into work, past the A and E ambulance bays and into the mini mall, she hadn't got the same thrill she was used to. She nodded to Mrs Lewis in the flowers and fruit shop, bought shampoo from the red-suited Miss Seddon in Foams. But there was no longer that feeling of being one of a team in Lizzie's.

It had been a dreary day and now she was filling in TTOs—To Take Out forms. These were the letters that were written for patients who were being discharged, to take to their GPs. They included details of diagnosis, treatment, important findings, drugs prescribed and follow-up care. All very important, of course, but there was a lot of copying out of details that were already on file. She was getting writers' cramp!

'Not superstitious, are you?' a voice asked.

She jerked at the sound of the voice—it was the last one she expected to hear. Her neatly arranged pile of papers fluttered to the floor and she leaned over to scrabble for them. It gave her a minute to collect her thoughts. What was Gray Woods doing back here?

'I thought you were in the Midlands for another ten days or so,' she mumbled. In fact, she knew it was exactly ten days. She had been counting them. Why had he come back early?

'You know how it is with hospital work when you're not exactly on the staff,' he said carelessly. 'You get to move about very easily. Why, have you missed me?'

She looked up. He was leaning, relaxed, on the wall of the doctors' room. He wasn't in his usual child-friendly working gear, but instead wore a dark formal suit, with the necessary white shirt and college tie.

'We could have done with you to help out,' she said gracelessly. 'Why are you dressed like that?'

'Formal clothes for a formal meeting. I've been having a few words with the consultant, and then we went to see Martyn Lennard—you know, the hospital manager. He's a good man; we had coffee together. But you didn't answer my question. Are you superstitious?'

'No,' she said caustically, 'I'm not superstitious. I don't touch wood, I do walk under ladders, I don't believe in the tooth fairy or my own personalised fairy godmother.'

What was wrong with her? she wondered. She was pleased to see him, why couldn't she show it? He must think she was...

'You've nearly finished,' he said, coming over to look at her pile of work. 'Leave the rest till morning. I've got something to show you—I want you to come with me.'

She frowned. 'Something to show me?'

He gave her no clue as to what he meant. 'Certainly. Now take off that tabard and get your coat. It's raining outside.'

She could finish now. It was late in the evening,

and she had been working quite a few late evenings recently. It seemed to be the only thing to do. 'Okay, let's go, then,' she said. She pulled on her anorak and the two of them went down to the ground floor. Through the glassed-in foyer, out to catch one of the many taxis. From somewhere he had picked up a coat, and, to her surprise, an umbrella.

'I didn't know you had an umbrella,' she said as he opened it to protect her from the stinging rain.

'I bought it last week. I felt I had to. I haven't got one in Australia, though. I have a sunshade there.'

'Don't tell me,' she said, the mention of Australia making her feel irritable again. 'Now where are we going?'

The rain drummed down on the umbrella. He stopped a taxi and handed her in. 'Westminster Bridge,' he told the driver, and stepped in beside her.

'Which side of the bridge, sir? Houses of Parliament?'

'No. Can you drop us right in the middle of the bridge?'

'If you want me to,' the man said doubtfully. 'But it seems a bit wet and dark to go sightseeing.'

'Not used to Australian lunatics,' Gray whispered to her, and she had to giggle.

The taxi eased down Park Lane, now not so crowded as it had been. She frowned. 'I want to know too—why the middle of Westminster Bridge?' she asked. 'And don't tell me it's not as fine as Sydney Bridge, I just don't want to know. I don't want to know about the sun shining all day either. It's been raining for three days now and I'm miserable because of it. And why ask me if I'm superstitious?'

'All will be revealed in a few minutes,' he told her. 'Sit there and contain yourself.'

She didn't know what to make of him. He seemed calmer than the last time she had spoken to him, as if some burden had been lifted from him. And there was an air of assurance about him, of certainty. Most pleasant of all, he was no longer speaking to her in that polite but absolutely detached way that so angered her. He was human again. The man she had…slept with. The man she loved.

The rain was harder than ever when they got to the middle of Westminster Bridge and climbed out. He held his umbrella over her, the rain rattling on it, silver drops running off the edge, splashing on the stone balustrade. 'What are we doing here?' she asked.

Calmly he replied, 'We're here because I love it. Look, the Thames below, Houses of Parliament there, there's no end of tradition, of history here. It's all wonderful.'

He was right, of course. Even—especially—in the March rain it was all wonderful. But… 'Gray Woods,' she said, 'it might be wonderful, but I'm standing here in the rain, tired, hungry, cold and now wet. There are not many men I would do it for. So now tell me why!'

He looked surprised. 'Didn't I tell you? We have to celebrate. I've booked a table for two, at a restaurant overlooking the river. I take it you are free?'

'I suppose so,' she said. 'Just what are we celebrating?'

'I told you, I've been talking to the hospital manager and the consultant. I'm taking a small drop in salary until I get a full-time post. I'm not going back to Australia, I'm staying at Lizzie's.'

Emotions surged through her breast, so many, so suffocating, she couldn't name them all. She was excited, shocked, jubilant, apprehensive, all at once. 'B-but I thought you wanted to go back,' she eventually managed to stammer. 'Why change your mind?'

'Well, there are more opportunities here, more chances of exciting work. And look around you, there's nothing quite like this in Australia. I've got quite used to England. I even like the crowds, like the fact that you can fly from one end of the country to the other in just a day. I want to stay. And I have to thank you for showing me so much.'

'Always glad to help,' she said dully. 'Can we go now?' Then anger flared through her. 'And why are you glad I'm not superstitious? What's it to you?'

'Well, I want to remember Australia. When I look at you. So I thought of something to remind me. You know we have the world's best opal mines?' He took a small box from his breast pocket, flicked it open. There was a simple gold band and mounted on it a great black opal.

'This is an opal engagement ring. Will you marry me, Lucy?'

Marry him? She was speechless. How could he ask her like this, just when she thought she'd lost him, without any lead-up, any hint whatsoever? The man was... Conflicting emotions warred inside her.

'Marry you! Gray Woods, you've never even said that you loved me!'

'Love you! You mad woman, of course I love you. I'll tell the world I love you. How could you ever doubt it? I fell in love with you the minute you pushed me into that green gunge. Of course I love you.' He paused, then asked gently, 'But do you love me, Lucy?'

She didn't answer at once. She listened to the rain rattling on the umbrella, felt the force of his arm round her, looked at the yearning in his eyes, visible even in the near darkness. There was the liquid movement of the river below them, the golden sight of the buildings behind them. What more wonderfully British place could there be for a proposal?

'Of course I love you, Gray Woods, and of course I'll marry you. There's no one I've ever wanted to marry more. Gray, you'll make me so happy!'

'If I can make you as happy as you've made me,' he answered.

HARLEQUIN®
INTRIGUE

WE'LL LEAVE YOU BREATHLESS!

If you've been looking for thrilling tales of
contemporary passion and sensuous love stories
with taut, edge-of-the-seat suspense—then
you'll love Harlequin Intrigue!

Every month, you'll meet four new heroes
who are guaranteed to make your spine tingle
and your pulse pound. With them you'll enter
into the exciting world of Harlequin Intrigue—
where your life is on the line
and so is your heart!

THAT'S INTRIGUE—
ROMANTIC SUSPENSE
AT ITS BEST!

HARLEQUIN®
Makes any time special ®

Harlequin Romance®

Delightful
Affectionate
Romantic
Emotional

Tender
Original

Daring
Riveting
Enchanting
Adventurous
Moving

Harlequin Romance® —
capturing the world you dream of...

HARLEQUIN®
Makes any time special ®

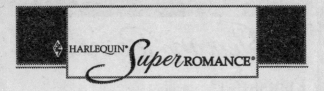

Harlequin® Historical

From rugged lawmen and valiant knights to defiant heiresses and spirited frontierswomen, Harlequin Historicals will capture your imagination with their dramatic scope, passion and adventure.

Harlequin Historicals . . . they're too good to miss!

HHDIR1